*The Last Librarian*

Osdany Morales

# THE LAST LIBRARIAN

Translated from the Spanish by Kristina L. Bonsager

**DALKEY ARCHIVE PRESS**

Originally published in Spanish by Letras Cubanas as *Papyrus* in 2012.

Library of Congress Cataloging-in-Publication Data
Names: Morales, O., 1981- author. | Bonsager, Kristina, translator.
Title: The last librarian / Osdany Morales ; translated by Kristina Bonsager.
Other titles: Papyrus. English
Description: First Dalkey Archive edition. | Victoria, TX : Dalkey Archive,
2017. | "Originally published in Spanish by Letras Cubanas as Papyrus in
2012" -- Verso title page.
Identifiers: LCCN 2017035401 | ISBN 9781628971811 (pbk. : alk. paper)
Subjects: LCSH: Authors--Fiction. | Libraries--Fiction. | Books--Fiction.
| Artists--Fiction. | Writing--Fiction. | Creation (Literary, artistic, etc.)--
Fiction.
Classification: LCC PQ7392.M4696 P3713 2017 | DDC 863/.7--dc23
LC record available at https://lccn.loc.gov/2017035401

www.dalkeyarchive.com
Victoria, TX / McLean, IL / Dublin

Dalkey Archive Press publications are, in part, made possible through the
support of the University of Houston-Victoria and its programs in creative
writing, publishing, and translation.

Printed on permanent/durable acid-free paper

# Index

**Book I: The Book of Writing**     14
THE SCRIBE

**Book II: The Book of Time**     40
TEMPO

**Book III: The Book of Perfection**     72
APROPOS OF THE WET SNOW

**Book IV: The Book of the Beast**     98
ETERNAL LOVE FOR JIM JARMUSCH

**Book V: The Book of Contemporaries**     122
FIGHT CLUB

**Book VI: The Book of Fame**     144
LOST IN TRANSLATION

**Book VII: The Book of the Book**     162
THE LAST LIBRARIAN

Since I can never see your face,
And never shake you by the hand,
I send my soul through time and space
To greet you. You will understand.

James Elroy Flecker

HOTEL ROOMS, ONLY A few square meters and a bathroom, a green, prairie-like rug you hesitate to walk on barefoot, the always-present minibar, a television with a parade of Smirnoff vodka commercials. Rows of seats at train stations. Waiting rooms in airports, where you think about the upcoming trip and life, while you contemplate the sky overhead that doesn't belong to the place you're going, nor to the one you just left. Mezzanines, lobbies with oversized vases, neoclassical funeral homes, rectangular swimming pools, hallways leading to theaters at cinema multiplexes. Escalators in art museums. Scholars' rooms at rigorous universities. Libraries: those accessible warehouses. Nine blank pages caused by a printing error in the middle of a book, such as *The Death of Virgil*. Margins of a printed page. Essays. The missing piece that makes unfinished works famous. Glass. Bars visited for the first time. Casinos, heirs of the Greek oracles. Train compartments and a connecting corridor in movies about fascism. The subway. Cats and migratory birds. All the vagabond dogs. Temporary work, temporary solutions. The faucet tied with a shoestring to stop it from dripping, continuing every day of the year. Centimeters of film left over after filming a scene. Empty ballpoint pens. Disposable syringes. The uterus, the appendix, baby teeth, late wisdom teeth. Childhood. Bridges. Wax statues. Hospitals, terrible fevers on stretchers, IVs. Window frames, the width of walls. Shopping-center garages, shopping centers. Rooftops of skyscrapers. Refugee camps. Non-political graffiti. The sea in international waters. Darkness signaled with a finger. Foreign prostitutes with whom you have short, practical conversations. A flag. A highway at night between continents. Essential city taxis and their immigrant drivers. Telephone booths and tele-

phones. Computer rooms. Trips, or rather, the distance from
one point to another, during which strangers and children ask
how much longer. Seven Libraries of the World and their Seven
Librarians. A text writing itself, like a whirlwind created by a
stray dog trying to bite its tail. A self-aware writing that re-
volves, whose framework is strengthened by fragments of its
own structure, which in turn supports itself on other fragments
of their own structure, and so on. A galaxy, at least, or a solar
system where the sun is interchangeably one of the planets and
then another and another. The orbits resume and bring light to
outer space on a whim. Children sitting in a circle, singing a
rhyme, and removing their boots from the circle to decide who
plays what in their game. Then imagining the seasons' changing
weather, the winds' direction and regularity, and the complexity
of destiny and broken dreams. The lack of function, uselessness,
the destiny of man.

This is the story of my journey to the Seven Libraries of the World. I started one morning in the twenty-first century, confident in my objective's clarity. I didn't announce my plans, nor did I consult with anyone. I didn't believe it myself until I realized I was quite far from where I'd started. At some point further on, the distance turned into unknown territories, where I lost and found new distances, and I made use of, as best I could, the time-honored methods of finding one's way.

Only once did I notice how isolated I was. I'd rested at a random hotel and after a long bath that steamed up the mirror, I slid the palm of my hand across the glass surface and discovered my face was that of a stranger. So this is the journey, I said to myself. I decided to call that stranger *me* and through his mirrored image I'll tell my tale.

The first place I spent the night was an inn called Calypso. I don't usually refer to it as part of the adventure because it's more associated with my departure from what, up until that point, had been the world than with the crusade I'd imposed on myself as part of a dream, initiation, or punishment. The inn belonged to a Frenchman, who every morning told me the same story about his missing friend.

According to his friend's letter, in a moment of carelessness the man had left his camera on a bus during a trip to Zurich. Since he'd been the only person on the bus and had confidence in Europeans' tact or distrust, as well as in the bus's punctuality, he felt obliged to wait for the same bus to return and see if his camera was still there. When he got on the bus again and walked to the seat where he'd nodded off, he confirmed his ideas about the Old World were not wrong. However, a few days later when he finished the roll of film and developed his photos, he found a sequence of three images he didn't recognize. The first was of an obscure neighborhood framed by the bus's glass window. The second held an image of an intersection, pedestrians, and trees in flowerbeds. The third, a little blurry, revealed the front of a house. The rest were photos of James Joyce's tomb and other symbolic sites his friend had visited during his tourist route. He'd never been to the part of the city shown in the unexpected images. He got back on the bus with the photos in hand. Sitting in the spot that seemed most like his previous seat, he waited and watched the unfamiliar streets of Zurich pass by. He came upon what might've been the area depicted in the first photo. He hoped he was wrong and completely confused, but then he glimpsed the corner with the same pedestrians and trees. He got off at the next stop and walked back, looking closely at the last photograph. He found the house in the middle of the block, after having mistaken it a few times for others along the continuous façade with identical, indistinguishable entrances. His ideas about the unchanging Old World were definitely not the same. It was as if the Europe he'd imagined as an enormous arthropod the size of an old mansion, which had died from lack of water, had, after being prodded several times with a branch to confirm its state of rigor mortis, twisted with a movement greater than the prodding, and slowly raised its legs, casting him in shadows and prepared to surround him. He walked up two steps and rang the bell, although he didn't hear it ring. At this point, the owner of Calypso always paused, opening his eyes wide, as if the story had ended or there was something he left for me to understand.

During my stay at the inn, I waited for something to keep me there. Since nothing happened, I was able to leave a few days later without regrets. To my advantage, however, I did begin my journey with two promising discoveries.

Scratched in the wooden window frame of my room, I found two short phrases. Judging by the handwriting, both were written by the same person. The letters' neatness didn't strike me as the result of a desperate gesture or a fit of lucidity, even less so a moment of boredom. Engraved with a tool or knife, the phrases caught my attention as cryptic messages, not easily seen on the window frame's exterior. From the window I could see a bridge and its meandering river, a red car parked behind a tree, and a blond model being photographed under the large reflectors. The model looked constantly at her watch, making me think she was a femme fatale preparing her alibi. *The center is unmoving, but miniscule*, was the inscription in the frame to the window's right side. I could only read the words with the heavy shutter completely open, after it squeaked its own version of the saying. In a symmetrical manner, on the other side, also protected by a closed shutter, I found: *Everything vanishes, but also endures.* The blond woman looked again at her watch and posed for the next photo.

"The city per se possesses an intrinsically utopian dimension by virtue of being situated outside the natural order." Boris Groys, I remembered.

At the back of a stationery shop in the city of Montevideo, I found the First of the Libraries. Two girls were writing in a school notebook before deciding which pen to buy.

"If you were to receive a love letter, what color ink would you prefer?" one of the girls asked me.

"What kind of love are we talking about?"

"It's a goodbye letter," announced the other girl.

"A love letter that's also a goodbye letter isn't such a complicated matter. Blue ink would work just fine."

"That's what I told them, but they didn't listen to me," said the shopkeeper. Then he leaned toward me a bit and added, "When a writer earns money with a book, he's bankrolling his time to write the next one. Nonetheless, there's always a first book written from borrowed time, others' support, or hunger."

"I ponder the rhythm of prose composed by a quill pen, which due to overuse needs to be dipped in ink before finishing a single line," I responded.

"The world is always greater than what one can imagine and smaller than it appears," replied the shopkeeper, who, without a doubt, was also the Librarian of the First Library.

"The center is unmoving, but miniscule," I told him, citing my hotel window frame.

"The old man on the other side would've liked that," he said. Walking around the counter, he climbed up on a high wooden chair and with his chin indicated an imaginary point in the distance. "The old man on the other side, the Masturbator."

I leaned forward a bit, looking in the direction he'd indicated, but I only saw the ordinary scenery of a colonial street.

"A little further that way, in Buenos Aires. The Great Masturbator! His stories are as close as you can get to one of

Picabia's machines. I can't claim that the Argentine hid some dirty magazine under his mattress, one without edges, silky as a Bible, or a book about sexual habits in the Balkan countries, but his story 'The Book of Sand' is a direct allusion to a passion for pornography. You don't believe me? The first line of the story, not even the first paragraph, is a simple preface that assures us of what'll come and as such supports my remark. But above all else it exonerates him from the passion of always having to add one more book to Literature. His first line warns us: *I live alone.* In other words, my friend: I am a masturbator. Immediately the protagonist receives a visit from a stranger, who introduces himself as a book salesman and suggests the writer purchase a Bible. Owing to his own knowledge, expertise on the subject, and general indifference, the protagonist rejects the suggestion, thus leading the salesman to show the man a different book, in contrast to what he usually sells. He recommends one that's completely opposite to all he's previously suggested. A book of the devil, a book of sand."

Pausing, the shopkeeper called to a woman who was entering the shop, "Hey, lady, what do ya want?" His raised voice frightened her and she left immediately. He then turned back to me, his face animated, and continued:

"An infinite text that doesn't possess a predictable narrative structure, order, nor obvious purpose except for the perverse pleasure of accumulating pages. The unusual book, you'll remember, contains among other things an anchor drawn by a child."

With a nearby pen, the shopkeeper quickly sketched an anchor on paper with old calculations scribbled in columns. He became distracted retracing the lines of the drawing, highlighting and deforming it while his thoughts wandered.

"It's odd that the salesman is far more passionate about his preference for Burns, the Scottish poet—who cultivated, along with his virtues, a reputation for being vicious and corrupt—

rather than Stevenson and Hume, those examiners of human nature. As the old perfectionist himself would've written, wanting, of course, to say something else: *I understood the book was monstrous.*"

"'It served me not at all to consider that I was any less monstrous,'" I concluded, reciting the text from memory.

"There you have it," said the shopkeeper. "Our man remains alone with the book of sand, while his reading destroys him with a hatred of humanity. He loses friends, reality, sleep, and his direction in life. The orgy of the chaotic book satisfies everything; moreover, he can't destroy the book and in the end abandons it in a library, as if he were throwing away his pornographic magazines or erasing all the lustful photos and files from his computer's hard drive in a fit of mutilation and presumed astuteness."

The shopkeeper crumbled up the paper where he'd drawn the anchor and threw it at the wastepaper basket behind his back, making the shot. Then it occurred to me to say:

"Everything vanishes, but also endures. Deep down he was a passionate man."

Maybe I took the risk to follow him in the game at this moment because I was distracted looking below the counter at some picture frames showing peaceful, out-of-date images of children and couples. The Librarian laughed, leaning on the chair as if he couldn't hold the weight of his laughter. Finally, he stood up, drying his eyes and shaking his head:

"Writers don't have depth, my friend. Of course, it's possible that I'm mistaken. It's also possible I've been left speechless more than once by the same thing that only appeared to be different. But because of this, I've become happier, even if I've been less wise. You can spend the night in the Library, but when you depart, you must leave a book so that the business flourishes."

Since I didn't have a book with me, I realized I'd have to write one while in the library.

"The twentieth century!" I heard him say, talking to himself. "We should preserve it and send it to a natural-science museum for children, as proof it did actually exist. What a crazy world." The girls were spinning a revolving shelf of postcards. From the hidden entrance of the southern library, I contemplated them for the last time. They were whispering, maybe imagining the love letter and the goodbye. I saw them immortalized in the golden landscape I observed behind them with the door framing the scene, as if it were a Renaissance composition. Montevideo and its nostalgic cynics, I thought. They didn't see me enter the First Library.

# Book I: The Book of Writing
## The Scribe

Leaving Becchina's songs behind, I paused in front of the candle. The slender flame danced before my eyes and at its base, drowning in a stream of wax, several motionless insects crackled.

"Grandmother, why do the beautiful spirits come to the fire to die?"

"Pierino, the beautiful spirits forget the world's cruelties."

Becchina caught me from behind and began to pull me toward her while she laughed, trying to frighten me. At that age I was too obedient to be devious. Although rebellion always inspires the emergence of precocious intelligence, my disciplined childhood immersed life in a clear, innocent past, in which time slipped by benevolently. My rebelliousness surfaced later, when I began to realize that I was rather intelligent. Practically being dragged into the shadows, I couldn't do anything to free myself from Becchina's arms.

"But Grandmother, the flame gives us light!" I called to her, but she didn't answer.

Becchina leaned close to my ear, so Grandmother couldn't hear her. "The butterflies die because we don't accept the shadows," she whispered. Then without resisting, I allowed her to take me to the darkest rooms.

For a long time Grandmother had been courted by Gian Galeazzo Visconti, who was the Duke of Milan and a daring businessman. Even though their relationship didn't exceed the excitement of adolescent flirtation, the incident impacted all subsequent history, at least all that concerned Grandmother. She'd been one of the most beautiful and fun-loving girls of Tuscany. Years later, withdrawn to more hardworking circumstances, you could still see moving through her fine features, hands, and hair, the spark that'd made Galeazzo notice her. In her old age, suffering from anxiety and having witnessed the decline of glorious times, she reminded us constantly of the duke's courtship. Consequently, when I think of my ancestors, I struggle to remember I'm not actually related to the Duke of Milan. In my memory he was a more important mythical figure than my loyal grandfather. When the duke died in 1402, Grandmother was busy mending an Etruscan tapestry. According to her, mending a tapestry had always been an omen of good fortune. Therefore, when she heard the sad news, she didn't abandon the fabric, but instead looked at the sunset and became even more engrossed with the battle's figures.

"I'm hoping for good news," she said.

Shortly thereafter they told her of my birth.


Becchina's breasts. She pretended to nurse me in the stables and I believed she did nurse me. At that age I was ready to believe anything. Becchina pulled me down into the hay and rubbed her nipples on my cheeks. One afternoon Brother Giuliano found us and that's when my lessons started.

"What is the body? The dwelling of the soul."

"What is light? The face of all things."

"What is the sun? The splendor of the world, the grace of nature, the provider of hours."

Each day Brother Giuliano was eager to confirm my progress. He was especially enthusiastic about my unique talent for writing. Rarely did I dare ask questions. I followed his movements with my eyes and put all my effort into advancing my training. I figured that once I'd passed all the tests and completed the lessons I could return to spending hours lying in the hay.

"Brother Giuliano, how do you write Becchina?"

Deep in thought, considering a prayer, he paused before responding.

"That word can't be written. It's not a word."

Since stubbornness wasn't present in my childhood disposition, at first I accepted what the priest said without trying to write letters to replicate the sounds. But it bothered me that Becchina's name, an utterance that calmed me, was considered a guttural mutant, a moan impossible to transform into lines on paper, a cursed phrase.

Common lines, geometry of soft angles, spots, smudges. I traced circles and spirals, caught sight of parallelisms in those drawings that seemed unorthodox to me, and condemned them to be scattered in the ashes. Folly. Ridiculous efforts. Hidden from the oil lamp's light, I continued tormenting myself, destroying pages as soft as cloth, where I'd tried time and again to discover the prohibited writing of her name, Becchina.

When I'd learned to write, I was sold to my uncle Carracci as a scribe. That morning when they sent me so far away, I didn't want to say goodbye to anyone and I cried silently the entire journey. I've never confessed that until today.

Carracci had lost his son in combat against the Duke of Milan and from time to time he rambled on about his loss. I suspected he often confused me with his son. Others told me of his dementia. He was cruel to me, not only because my appearance confirmed his delirium, but I was also the living image of the deception.

To spend a moment gazing longingly at the horizon toward the path that'd led me to his castle, I had to hide. I thought about Grandmother's last words and scribbled guesses at the spelling of Becchina's name everywhere.

I awoke dutifully each morning and promptly started my walk to the library. Those first days I enjoyed trailing my hand against the wall, leaving behind a line that affirmed an idle certainty of my progression from sleep to work, the principal purpose for my stay under Carracci's control. I'd heard some stories about him, all of them quite fierce, and writing his memoirs comforted me. In spite of being far from Becchina, I felt that my work, if nothing else, received the secret support of my loved ones.

Each morning as I entered the gallery, I saw his rigid back, which looked like a portal that could only be opened with great effort. Everything about Signore Carracci was severe. He was neither short, nor tall, but of average height. He wore a shabby, red coat that reached his feet; the lined sleeves were rolled up. He sat motionless, crestfallen, and lost in his memories as if he'd arrived early to review in his mind the events that he'd later dictate to me in a clear and abundant flood of thought. Instead of engaging with each of his life's accomplishments, it seemed he merely read from an invisible book. Fascinated by his eloquent speech, I also understood why he chose not to have a biographer, who would've revised or praised these episodes differently than he or who, in the worst case, would've maintained a guarded difference of character or religious conviction.

The sunlight brilliantly pierced the gallery's arches, creating a sequence of seashells on the floor, which I desecrated with my footprints. Then I broke the perfect lines of the arches by throwing my shadow upon them. In those few moments of joy, I witnessed the miracle of creating something beyond myself and became an attentive observer of man and nature's achievements. When I finished working, the sun had already crossed to the other side of the castle and the images of the seashell arches were replicated on the wall, where all I could do was add my silhouette, exhausted from so much writing.

Despite the terrible things that happened later, Carracci was a clearheaded man, who dedicated his energies to the cult of the mind. He wasn't passionate about falconry or hunting, as could be expected of someone of his stature. With the loyalty of a servant, he walked the halls and rooms of his domain every day and spent hours in the library, although I only saw him open a book once.

His library was exceptional. There I found the teachings of Thomas Aquinas and Albertus Magnus, and great thinkers like Aristotle and his critics. Also represented were Latin poets, whom I could appreciate thanks to Brother Giuliano's teachings, and many letters from Catherine of Siena, great founders of the Church, Greeks and Romans, Gregorio, Basilio, Ignacio, and Origen. To my dismay, I found them to be simpleminded and complimentary of irrelevant vocations. Nowhere in my readings did I find a word similar to Becchina.

"They belonged to my son," he confessed the morning that I caught him paging through one of the books. He seemed to be embarrassed. That day he didn't dictate a single exploit. Instead, he moved toward me and let loose a right-handed punch so powerful it knocked me to the floor.

"Get up."

I stood up without even understanding what the violence had meant. I remember thinking about my Grandmother's face and felt sad. I was straightening my disheveled clothing and brushing off the dust from the floor when he hit me again.

"Get up."

And again I stood up, clumsily. I pitied myself for the disciplined part of me that obeyed more out of an idealized image of who I was than out of respect for Carracci. He hit me so many times, until one time while I was sprawled on the floor, I realized I was capable of lying.

"I can't," I said. "I can't get up, Uncle."

I saw the red of his coat move into the distance, the hem twisting as it skimmed the floor. I stood up, pulled myself together, and brushed off the dirt, careful to avoid touching all the places that hurt. Then I took refuge among the books.

One morning while I was writing down the story of a battle, I discovered that his madness created within him two distinct people and that sometimes he could be exceptionally kind to me.

"Leave that there, Pierino," he said, "and come over to the window."

I assumed he wanted to show me something or blame me for some mess that I'd be able to see from there. He placed his hand on my shoulder, which just brushed up against the windowsill, and he began an account worthy of his memoirs, disclosing one of his combat techniques. I remember it, more or less, like this:

"In battle against the enemy rider, there will always be two potential targets for the attack: the rider and the horse. Choosing the first will put an end to the danger and the horse will return at full gallop to where they await news of the rider's death. The second choice, disloyal and sinister, will decrease the threat and secure a new battle in which one could quickly be defeated, if one trusts too much in the merit of the first attack. Or, to consider the other side of the scenario, one could see his stature reduced if the other rider then kills the opponent's horse and must face the enemy in the same condition. In that case, the only secret advantage the rider maintains is that only one target remains to attack."

At first I thought he was asking forgiveness for having kept me so far from my loved ones, but later I suspected that he was confessing his fears. Without realizing it, he gave me a strategy of revenge. He who can see how much there is to win in a battle cannot help but desire it. He who doesn't have a battle doesn't have a victory. And he who doesn't have a victory is lost.

The pain from the blows kept me from sleeping, while the swelling of my face and side made breathing difficult. Suddenly, I was aware that a hand brushed my sweaty hair from my forehead, feeling for signs of a fever. I stopped moaning, partly from fear and curiosity, partly due to the gentle warmth that hand promised me. It smelled of wax and oils. Maybe the person held a candle, but I didn't want to, or couldn't, open my eyes.

"Becchina?" I murmured, demanding a favor from fate. The hand pulled away in fear.

"Becchina!"

I saw the silhouette vanish into the room's darkness. Its hasty retreat caused the candle's dull light to flicker, leaving me in the dark once the shadow withdrew against the walls. Moving forward, I felt a mixture of sorrow and happiness.

"Becchina," I whispered as if I were calling a cat. "Becchina."

I scoured the corners where I'd seen the ghostlike figure hide, but found nothing more than shadows. Stumbling on an uneven part of the floor that began a large staircase, I nearly lost my balance. I returned to the window and opened it to allow the night's shadows, which are finer than the wall's shadows, to reveal the secrets I'd been unable to glimpse on my own.

The stairs led to a narrow hallway that in turn led to a center point from which three passages radiated. The middle passage appeared to be a continuation of the path to my room. It ended, as one would expect, in the library.

After emerging from behind a tapestry, it took me a long time to recognize the room I'd just entered. Illuminated by the moon's light, the room looked different and I assumed it was a cave. I thought I'd discovered another library, but then I saw my papers that I worked on daily resting on the table and understood this was the room of my work and torture. I realized I'd been given the room of my Uncle Carracci's son.

I returned to the passages, approached the center, and explored the path to the right. This passage seemed endless. Setting aside my fear, I put both hands on the humid walls. Stairs kept appearing suddenly in front of me and one misstep by my legs, still suffering from the inflicted pain, could've sent me falling into a small hell.

The animal yielded to my caresses. It took a few steps and lowered its head. I stroked its mane gently and it shivered as if a bad thought had frightened it. The stable air reminded me of another stable and the summer afternoons before my lessons with Brother Giuliano started and I was transformed into a valuable commodity.

"Horses are the irrational side of the warrior," my Grandmother said as she finished a story about the Duke. In silence I used to scoff at her words, because the horse always seemed an odd animal. Its hide shudders without objection to a gentle breeze, then later it rears up against imaginary enemies. I suppose horses possess an awareness when facing danger that is different than what the rider feels. Doesn't its neigh sound like an apocalyptic warning? They are definitely not clever animals, nor are they enthusiastic about commands or maneuvers dictated by kicks to the abdomen. Even the wildest horses lower their muzzles to eat from a trainer's hand.

I moved my hand close to the horse's nostrils and waited for its timid breath. With its tail it flicked away a fly and then shifted to one side. From behind its back, Becchina appeared.

When the swelling left my face, I couldn't see anything. I'd had to wait several days for the skin to lose its bluish-purple color and for the normal earthy color to appear again. However, when the inflammation receded and my eye reappeared, everything was still blurry. I could only see out of my left eye.

Every morning as I crossed the arched hall to the library, I struggled to judge the distance between the wall and my hand, which I used to draw an imaginary line. I felt my way along the hall, step by step, and sometimes came so close to the wall that I scraped my knuckles. At the writing table, the point of the reed pen kept digging into the paper, causing me to carve jagged holes. I had to search my previous knowledge of my fingers to calibrate the distance between myself and everything else. Nonetheless, at night when I tried to solve the riddle of the forbidden name, the strokes became clearer and from the depths the name came closer to my waking thoughts. Be that as it may, this increasing closeness to the solution didn't distract me from revenge.

Now familiar with the path, as if it were an invisible string connecting the library to my room, I set forth every night on the journey back. No longer seeking to find Becchina's apparition, looking instead for Carracci's writings. During the mornings and afternoons, I labored to transcribe the master's arrogant words, but at night I wrote the words of my rebellion. Later, I carefully destroyed the original manuscripts and in their place inserted shameful evidence of a stingy and miserable life.

My strategy was conceived when I began to suspect that Carracci didn't know how to read, or else he wouldn't have needed a scribe. The only reason I even wrote down his words was because the act of destroying his memoirs was the worst rebellious act I'd ever committed. I lugged the manuscripts to the underground rooms, where I burned them. I then retraced my steps to the room I'd taken over and there I began creating humiliations and cowardly deeds to sully his legacy. I took advantage of all the stories my Grandmother had told me to find material to mock Carracci's former lovers and relatives. No one knew the story of his life better than I did, and no one was in a better position to tarnish it.

Into his narratives, I incorporated phrases I took word for word from books in the library to make him appear guilty of plagiarism and the most shameful imitation of his contemporaries, as well as of writers from several previous centuries. The events, which had previously been dictated by a virile and warlike god, were in this new version the product of an injured and cyclopean author—me. It was as if my one eye were only able to see foolishness and greed. Thus, his greatest defeats appeared to be of his own doing, as opposed to his adversaries' strength. I assigned the honors of his strategies to the most anonymous soldiers. He was stripped of his wisdom regarding love and gambling. I blamed him indirectly for my parents' deaths and added dangerous confessions against the Roman Church and various Florentine authorities. To do this I employed the most raucous-sounding words, which reminded me of a wetland full of frogs when I read them aloud. Amid the pain, my soul took pleasure and celebrated, for between the thorns it perceived the scent of the rose about to blossom.

Brother Giuliano took me to the far side of the castle, so I wouldn't be present when they carried out Carracci's body.

"Pierino!" he said to me, placing a hand on my shoulder. "There are days that offer proof of another world." I leaned against a column, as if one of us could quietly collapse.

"Giuliano, where will this column end up one day?"

Lifting his hand from my shoulder, he caressed the column's curved surface. He looked up toward its crown and the connecting arches. I followed his gaze with my eyes.

"This column can't leave here, Pierino. This is its time."

I slept the whole way in the wagon, stretched out on the hay. It was almost night when we arrived. Brother Giuliano reached under my arms to help me down, but I avoided him and jumped to the ground on the other side. I saw him walk to the stable leading the horse. What is light? The face of all things. What is man? A possession of death, a pedestrian who passes by, a guest who belongs to where he is.

By a window, begging the day for its last traces of light, my Grandmother sat weaving. I'd thought when the moment arrived my voice would fail me, an agonizing sound would escape my lips, and I would fall dead from love. But I was tired, sad, and withered. Grandmother put down the tapestry and turned toward me, which also took effort.

"What good news do you have for me?" she asked.

The sunset's glow disappeared as if it'd waited for the moment when Grandmother ignored it to leave us in the shadows. Becchina arrived and obediently began lighting the candles one by one. Without looking at me even once, she slipped out of the room after delivering the flame. I remained motionless, looking at my Grandmother's form, caressed by the candlelight. I was very hungry, and my skin smelled of manure and hay. My back still hurt from the bruise. I was blind in one eye. After holding the reed pen so much, my right hand had become deformed and looked like a raven's wing. Carracci was dead. And Becchina hadn't greeted me, she'd changed. She seemed to call herself by another name.

Grandmother awaited my reply, "What good news do you have for me?"

"I've returned, Grandmother."

Near the closest candle, I could see an insect hovering, then it met its end in the wax.

The next day a pregnant Becchina escaped with Brother Giuliano. Thinking back to a strange noise, I remember having been waken at sunrise by kicks and a neighing sound. In that instant, still in my dreams, I'd finally written her name on the dusty floor. In the morning nothing was left.

*

In a Shanghai mall, I met a European girl, who resembled a teenager's sketch of a girl on her school notebook's back cover. We'd followed similar paths in the mall. She'd lingered a few times and then I impulsively intercepted her cart in the middle of an aisle. On the back of her short dress was an image of Mikhail Gorbachev. She said she'd bought it because the expression on his face reminded her of one of her neighbors, who was the most inappropriate man she knew. This made me wonder how I could become an inappropriate man and if, having succeeded in getting her to remove one of the earphones to her iPod, I was in fact being inappropriate. She explained that the dress alluded to the generation that had Roman Polanski instead of Harmony Korine and the repulsive Charles Manson instead of Marilyn Manson. We paused so she could dig through a display of Italian pastas, looking for a certain type with a particular form, not cylindrical, nor flat, nor spiraled. After finding the one she was looking for, she took a moment to confirm she had the right one. I took a package of the same pasta to see if the search was really worth the effort.

Mala had lived in France after her parents left Belgrade in 1993, when she was four years old. As the escalator carried us upward, she stood in front of me contemplating the roof's aerodynamic structure. I figured the image on her back resembled her inappropriate neighbor more than the Nobel Peace Prize-winning Gorbachev.

Stopping in front of a Converse shoe display that filled an entire wall, she informed me that the brand was celebrating its one-hundred-year anniversary.

"It was founded in 1908," she said, "and now they're celebrating having put shoes on feet all over the world, including

Chuck Taylor, James Dean, John Lennon, Magic Johnson, and Elvis. Just imagine the excitement of walking through the *Belle Époque*. The unbecoming streets of 1908. Dublin in 1908. Paris in 1908. Massachusetts in 1908. In Vienna that year, the Austrian architect Adolf Loos gave his talk 'Ornament and Crime,' which basically accelerated the arrival of the Modernist movement, or at least these little white boxes," she said touching her iPod as if to assure me, in case I thought she was lost, that she knew exactly where her lecture was headed.

"Cavafy," she continued, "wrote the splendid poem 'Days of 1908.' In Michigan, also in 1908 of course, Alfred Day Hershey was born. Years later he became the geneticist who proved that a virus's nucleic acid could transmit genetic information and then replicate more viral particles inside a bacteria. All that sounds quite libidinous, but it's basically one step closer to opening the door to that well-known friend we affectionately call DNA. As a narrative element, DNA functions the same in science fiction as it does in melodramas about hidden paternity. In 1908 the Wright brothers certainly didn't fly for the first time; they'd already done that five years prior for a few seconds in North Carolina. However, in our year of Converse, the two brothers flew with their first passenger, in a flight that lasted six minutes and twenty-four seconds. That was also the first year in which a passenger died, but it wasn't the same passenger. In New York Alfred Stieglitz and Edward Steichen founded Gallery 291, where their exhibitions raised the profile of photography to the level of art, despite the many critics who considered it simplistic. Also that year, Henri Cartier-Bresson was born, as was Claude Lévi-Strauss, who was so influential last century that it's enough to simply list his splendid titles."

Mala then proceeded to recite the anthropologist's bibliography while she picked up all the shoes on the display one by one and then returned them to their places:

"*Tristes Tropiques, The Raw and the Cooked, The Origin of*

*Table Manners, From Honey to Ashes, The Naked Man,* and
*The Savage Mind.* Another interesting title from 1908 was *The
Unmasking of Robert-Houdin* by the magician Harry Houdini,
who seemed to prove there's no afterlife. Or if there is, that it's
unexplainable or erases our memory. Edmondo De Amicis died
in 1908. Enough said."

I remembered having seen the cover of an old edition of his
book *Heart: An Italian Schoolboy's Journal* and decided to trust
her on the subject.

"In 1908," she continued, "when the beloved painter
Edvard Munch was hospitalized because of anxiety, he'd already
painted *The Scream, The Sick Child,* and *The Dance of Life.*
Also in 1908, as determined by Alfred Nobel in his will, the
Royal Swedish Academy of Sciences awarded British physicist
Ernest Rutherford for his atomic structure discoveries, which
later stained history with what became the mushroom cloud.
Gaston Gallimard, along with others, founded in 1908 *La
Nouvelle Revue Française,* which developed into the illustrious
publishing house where the likes of Proust, Breton, Camus,
and Sartre paraded their works. In 1908 Henry Ford's company
started production of one of its most famous automobiles, of
which twenty years later it'd sold fifteen million . . . copies?
Later, they sold eight thousand B-24 bombers for the second
season of the international war-themed series. The famous
Oskar Schindler was also born in 1908 and O. Henry wrote
*The Voice of the City.* Also in 1908 Braque and Picasso kept
themselves busy creating a series of landscapes with a Cézanne
flair, which after a critic's contagious phlegm came to be called
Cubism. At the start of the twentieth century, there were only
twelve Indian rhinoceroses, which are identifiable by their
single horn. In 1908 the Kaziranga National Park was formed
to protect these outrageous unicorns. Hilda Doolittle and Ezra
Pound discovered the depths of haiku in 1908. Puyi, the last
emperor of China, was born in 1908; his story is best told by

film director Bertolucci. Georges Sorel published *Reflections on Violence* in 1908, which didn't fall into a void; on the contrary, it fell into the hands of several politicians, including Vladimir Ilyich Lenin. Some even considered it a good book. G. K. Chesterton published *The Man Who Was Thursday* in 1908 and it was read by the Argentine writer Borges. Born in 1908 was the Italian writer Cesare Pavese, who left us those fiery verses in *Death Will Come and Will Wear Your Eyes*, only later to commit suicide in a hotel room shortly after winning a literary prize."

"'That day we too will know that you are life and you are nothingness,'" I remembered aloud.

"Oh, the days of 1908," sighed Mala, "days in which a person, simply to say something, to commemorate a yearning, or to focus on a slight regret, put on a pair of these shoes for the first time!"

On the terrace on the shopping mall's upper floor, we found an empty café. She went ahead to claim a table at the far end, where we could watch the landscape of parked cars, as if it were farmland. I looked again at Gorbachev's face during her rush to the table, until Mala turned around and invited me to take the other seat. It seemed to me that everything about her was like a French playing card, but instead of the reversible face on both halves, she revealed two opposite figures, harmonious and contradictory at the same time. In a shopping center in Shanghai, looking for the Second Library and accompanied by a Serbian girl who seemed to be drawn by hand, the suggestion of playing cards wasn't that odd.

"I have few memories of Belgrade," she said after we ordered two cappuccinos. The waiter, an older man, seemed uncomfortable and quickly returned to the bar. He was probably imagining what he'd do if his daughter came home one afternoon wearing a dress with Mao Zedong on the back:

"Oh, dad, please, it's in fashion. Soon it'll sit in my closet with the other clothes I don't use anymore." He'll think that the short dress shows a lack of respect. And she'll defend it saying she'd bought it with prize money she'd won in a national poetry contest. The father will rebuke what he considers a cynical act, or even a cruel one, that she feels nothing wrong about wearing that dress. Then she'll say that it makes her feel cooler and like she's walking barefoot on the Red River banks. She keeps this last part to herself though, because of its counterproductive poetic effect. He might start screaming that in his house such a rag may not be worn. And his daughter, to avoid irritating him by saying that he's calling the leader's image a rag, instead packs her suitcases and moves to an apartment far away. Thus, the waiter decided he wouldn't say anything to his daughter if he saw her that night wearing such a dress. Then he brought the cappuccinos to our table.

"Actually, I believe I have only one memory," said Mala. "I'm with other kids on a carousel set between huge, old houses, or at least they seemed huge to me then. I was wearing mittens that made me uncomfortable, because they didn't have five separate finger holes, but rather one for the thumb and a second for the other fingers, like an oven mitt. In the freezing temperatures, the threads of the mittens stuck to the metal tube I was holding onto. The enchanted roofs of the houses spun, while the children's faces stayed still, caught in a scene with the background spinning behind them. Of course, it doesn't really mean anything. It's not an image from an anthology of children's drawings from difficult times, but that carousel is my only memory of Belgrade."

I asked her if she'd returned. She replied gazing at the colorful cars: "Belgrade! When someone says the name of a city very slowly, it always sounds like she's missing the place. It could just be for theatrical effect, but think about it. As the person looks inward, her eyes change as if watching it rain and announce the name: Berlin, Salt Lake, 1908 . . . And the declaration opens a dark hole, and inside is the city. However, the disclosure is also a decoy, seeking to place blame for her uprooting. The invocation of a place or time is merely testing to find out if that city, that street, that year are truly buried behind a stone wall."

She drew an earthy-colored spiral in her cappuccino's foam as she stirred it. Attempting to mock the tone she'd just used, she laughed.

"Everything vanishes, but also endures," she said, making a face as if she'd just said something very obvious, an overused phrase or obsolete saying. "I'm going to give you a test," she said, smiling. Skeptical, I kept silent.

"You're a university student . . ."

"To do this test, should I think like a student in my current situation or like the time when I was a student?"

"It's only a scenario, think like you do now, but you're a scholarship student at the university, OK?"

"OK."

"You're going to the cafeteria and it's near closing time. There's no one left, just a few lights and a line of women in white uniforms serving the food, while you slide your tray down the metal countertop."

"What kind of university is it?"

"It doesn't matter. You have your tray in your right hand and a glass of water in the other. In the middle of all the empty tables, you see a guy seated by himself eating."

"But of course."

"First question: do you go sit with him and keep him company or do you sit alone?"

"First, I pause while holding the tray in my right hand and drink a sip of cold water, while I consider the available tables. I look over my shoulder at the cafeteria ladies, who are watching for my decision. And I see you moving behind them, observing without being seen."

"And then?"

"I sit alone at an empty table."

"OK. At a table close to the guy or close to where you are standing?"

"I sit directly behind him."

"I think you're a dangerous guy."

"Is that what your test says?"

"It's what your eyebrows say."

"They say that? Here's a question, is the food on the tray awful?"

"Yes, but the guy eats it. I don't see why you couldn't do the same."

"I don't know. I think that maybe tonight I'll kill the guy."

"Why? Make something up. Did he steal your girlfriend?"

"No."

"Well, I don't know. Tell me why."

"That guy is me when I was eighteen years old and the last thing I'd want to do is sit with him. We're so different and yet so similar. There are a few things I didn't know how to do. Luckily the cafeteria ladies see him finish his food and they make the tray disappear through a hole in the wall, while he gets more water. After slowly drinking it and looking at the ocean of tables, he'll stick his hands in the pockets of his worn jeans and disappear without noticing me."

As we finished our cappuccinos, it seemed natural to make small talk. She jumped ahead:

"Don't ask me what I'm doing here, because you'll never believe it."

I thought about my far-fetched undertaking, the adventure of the Seven Libraries, and told her she wouldn't be able to swallow any of my motives that made our meeting possible. Mala was visiting countries. She was a filmmaker and wanted to find the exact point between Chris Cunningham and Michel Gondry. It wasn't clear to me whether she was referring to the dreamlike elements or twistedness of their work. Without hesitation, she probably would've responded, "Both." Trying to provoke her, I questioned whether she wasn't too young to have such clarity about life and she asked me not to say that again.

"There's nothing worse than an *enfant terrible*," she said.

"One time I saw an experimental video that I haven't been able to forget," I told her. "On the screen you see some animals, including a camel and a lion, and you hear the narrator's voice explaining that he'd found vintage films his grandfather had shot of zoo animals. While we watch the close-ups of animals, the narrator explains that while studying the reels he was surprised by the precision of his grandfather's work, especially how the narration and close-ups were always the same length. He then tells how he went to work with film producer Peter Greenaway. When he arrived in the city where they were to film, he found out that the work on *Prospero's Books* was delayed and would be rather informal. The producer suggested he take advantage of the free days, so he spent his time filming and familiarizing himself with the natural areas where he'd work sometime in the near future. He introduces us to these weightless film fragments as he narrates his mini-adventures, appearing to follow a plan, and incorporates numerous blank screens. At one point, he visits a zoo, where they film some scenes for the movie. Two kids guide him around, showing him the animals and suggesting certain routes. At one moment, while we're looking at typical zoo scenes, he tells us that one of the elephants has fallen in the sand. He covers the lens with another blank screen. He explains that in such a situation the animal becomes terribly anxious about trying to right itself and kicks in vain, which can result in a heart attack. In this particular occurrence, the caretakers ran to put bundles of grass near the elephant, forming little by little a more solid surface to help the elephant stand up. They did this with great urgency, because they feared the elephant's constant trunk-twisting and leg-agitating would increase its heart rate. While the workers were placing the bundles, the elephant died suddenly of a heart attack after an intense frenzy of energy. All of this we were told while looking at a blank screen. Later we returned to the bland scenes and the narrator shares that he's worried about having filmed the whole thing. The material puts him in a moral dilemma. He has recorded an event never before captured with such authenticity, but at the same time it shows a terrible combination of the victim's horror and the spectator's cruelty. He doesn't know what to do with the scene. A few days later, filming started for the movie that had originally brought him there. I don't remember how the video continues, but at the end you see a boy walking in a field beside his grandfather. The credits scroll through and then in the last seconds we see the bars of the elephant enclosure and a large elephant stretched out on the ground. In complete silence we watch the urgency of the caretakers running to put straw under his feet, near his belly, and along the curve of his back. We're torn whether we should watch or look away, but you have to see it because you can't do anything else. Curiosity and morbidity are relentless. While we watched, the elephant, in an intense frenzy of energy, overcame the lethargic sand and got to its feet, rising to its full height and splendor, unlike anything I'd ever witnessed before."

Mala had visited most of the same countries I had. She'd only seen elephants in China. During the five weeks she was in Shanghai, she'd gone several times to a small zoo there. I asked her to tell me about the last country she'd visited.

"Cuba? It's an unusual place," she said. "Only there can you go to a store to buy adhesive paper for windows and while you're trying to decide between the various options, the salesman will tell you how to make the windows opaque without applying the plastic coating that's displayed on the shelves behind him. The method is easy. You take a piece of glass, wrap it in a handkerchief, and crush it with the heel of a shoe or with a grinder as if it were a piece of garlic. When it becomes a fine powder, you rub it on the glass surface, using a piece of cardboard. Remember to get the corners and try to maintain equal pressure the whole time.

Little by little the window becomes opaque from the particles scraping on the glass. And you learn this from the same person who makes his living from selling window adhesives. What do you think of that?"

"Amazing," I said, just to say something. I was still thinking about my elephant.

"Another thing that baffles me is how they use the word *compañero*," she said. "They use it as if they were saying *señor* or *señora*, in a show of basic camaraderie. But over the years the word has lost all community affiliation and it's used more for strangers. When you want to get the salesperson's attention, you say: *Compañero*, followed by whatever you want to say. If you want to ask for directions, you address the person as *compañero* and he most likely will mention several other *compañeros* . . . he doesn't have the slightest idea who they are. One day on the Malecón esplanade in Havana, I passed a young local girl and an older European man. The girl, who appeared completely charmed by the man, hugged him and said: 'Oh, how fabulous, *compañero!*'"

In the hotel while Mala slept and Gorbachev's image resembled a flag tossed on the floor, I prepared the pasta that did actually seem to have something special about it. I looked through her iPod without waking her and found the sequel of *Pirates of the Caribbean*, which I hadn't seen. I sat on the bed beside her and watched the movie for a while. A little before it finished, she woke up, moved closer to me, and said something that seemed to be from a dream:

"Reading only the poète maudit isn't reading all literature."

"That could be," I said.

She motioned for me to give her one of the earphones and nonchalantly proceeded to tell me the rest of the movie. Afterward we had sex again. I dreamed I visited Belgrade, but later it was Havana, where in a park surrounded by shelves a salesman resembling Jack Sparrow offered me a book of photographs of

Che Guevara. All the images in the book were of Mala, naked in different poses. In one photo she was preparing spaghetti, wearing an apron with a scene of parked cars resembling a farm field. On the last page, she was on the back of a gray elephant and was saying goodbye, which is impossible to do in a photo.

The Second Library, constructed in the ruins of a German factory, was located in an old railway building. The steel beams rose like the skeleton of an abandoned submarine against the Munich sky. A few sturdy plants struggled to stay alive, their mostly green leaves contrasting with the patina of another time. Through the soot on the large windows, I could see the wool yarn still threaded on the long rows of looms, as if suspended in time. On the stairs of a brick building across the street, a boy hopped on one foot, holding the other behind him. Now and again he glanced at me to make sure he still had an audience.

"In the center of this Library," said the Librarian, who appeared to be a scientist who'd just returned from buying a post-war newspaper, "where the corridors intersect, are what remains of a much-admired central patio surrounded by columns. These days the patio can be difficult to find. In one of the corners sits a black toad sunning himself; he's the gatekeeper. If you can manage to sustain a conversation with the toad until he jumps into the pool, you'll be allowed to continue on to the rooms, where you can rest. However, before you depart, you must leave a new book."

All the labyrinthine corridors, at some point, led to the factory's center. Through the fine ironwork of the colonnade, I could clearly see the toad. I hung around the edge of the pool and waited for him to speak. He closed and opened his eyes as if the air bothered him and then said:

"Long ago painting and architecture apprentices were forced to replicate models in considerable detail on canvas or paper. The purpose was to remove their desire to create and to minimize the passionate impulses that are so common in youth, leaving them instead to concentrate on techniques detached from any excitement induced by an image yet to be conceived. The master artists obviously had little or no confidence that the adolescents would experience admiration upon encountering a work of art. Or, on the other hand, maybe they feared for the new students' fate in their rushed encounter with total darkness. The most precocious apprentices broke their paintbrushes, while the others masturbated in silence and then got rid of any evidence."

"Masturbation as proof of fertility," I responded, "where there's no opportunity for irreverence nor cosmogonies, for faith nor lack of faith, but above all else, it's an act of fictionalizing desire, desire itself."

"The art academies should also teach the students a trade," said the toad. "When you look at a studio, you know only one artist, or at most three, will create a memorable work. Therefore, by not also training them in precious metalwork, masonry, or carpentry, we commit an act of cruelty and condemn them to a life in limbo, floating endlessly on the air currents like seabirds."

"Just because a person doesn't know for whom he writes, it doesn't mean he writes for himself," I said.

"Centuries ago an author's wisdom and time were his own," said the toad. "In his writings, he established absolute knowledge of the world, but today that's impossible. Now the author begins from his intuition, because he's unaware of how much he knows. His knowledge resembles an Asian painting, in which a branch and a small boat drift alongside a void. The oarsman looks to both sides and sees nothing but emptiness."

"In a town not too close nor too far from Beijing," I said, "the ownership of objects was very powerfully connected to knowing their names. When a man sold an object to another, he had to disclose the name of the artifact and, bound by a thousand-year-old code of honor, he then had to forget it immediately and never again utter the word until the day he acquired the object again. Often thieves waited until the moment when the word was stealthily whispered near the new owner's ear. Or they extracted the word from the frightened owners, but in this case the owners usually lied and the object returned to them a few days later at their estate doors. Affluent people contracted a host of calligraphers to whom they assigned one syllable each of an object's name. Consequently, the seller told the buyer which calligraphers and in which order their syllables would produce the exact combination for the object's proper name. If a man were swindled in a deal and given an object's false name, it was easily proven, because when the false name was used, the object began to alter its appearance. The most miserly people, and thus the most frequently tricked, walked through their galleries every morning and named their objects one by one, to confirm the authenticity of their purchases. Consequently, several were robbed by thieves with fine listening abilities, while other owners clumsily confused the words and saw their acquisitions fade away under an erroneous name."

"The case of Li is frequently mentioned," said the toad, "as someone who experimented with the objects he acquired. On one occasion he began calling a group of diverse objects by the same word. With time the objects resembled one another and the differences were only visible to him. Then, he began to return their original names to them and the objects reverted to their unique shapes. This sculptor was banished from the village without a single belonging, not even his statues, which the people considered demonic and crushed beneath enormous boulders."

"The story continues that Li, exiled in the woods, repeated one by one the names of his objects and recovered all of them before his death. This village didn't produce any poets. Those who made the greatest efforts left only blank lines where they repeated thing, thing, thing, and other vague terms lacking definitions," I concluded.

"The center is unmoving, but miniscule," said the toad.

"Everything vanishes, but also endures," I said.

The toad jumped into the dark pond, his back shining below the water like a shooting star.

# Book II: The Book of Time
# Tempo

# I

THE CARRIAGE CAME ABRUPTLY to a halt with a curse from the coachman. The horses' front hooves descended around me, as they shook their halters and snorted in protest.

"I'm not a thief," I shouted. "The law is after me because of a misunderstanding and I've no choice but to leave Italy."

The coachman turned in his seat, apparently to receive orders. He faced forward again, but didn't say a word. Then the small door opened. Not waiting for a formal invitation, I hopped into the carriage as the sounds of the horses' hooves mixed with the grinding of the large, metal wheels.

"One could say I'm an admirer of the misunderstood," she said as a way of greeting. "My name is Margarita and while you are within these two doors, you'll be safe."

The interior of the coach, in contrast to what the outside measurements indicated, seemed excessive in comparison to a common carriage.

"Relax," she said. "You've stumbled upon a suitable coach."

Despite the voice of a mature woman, she looked like an eleven-year-old girl. It made my head spin to reconcile the idea that the shrill voice and calmness with which she expressed her logic corresponded to the wax-like, childish body dressed in fine cloth that was Margarita. Through the window I saw tree trunks pass by. Occasionally light entered, revealing the mysterious satchel I was trying to hide.

"Do you have friends in France?"

"I've never had anyone anywhere," I responded. "I'm going to France because if I stay on this side it won't be long before they find me, and who knows how I'll end up."

"You won't know that being on the other side either," said Margarita without taking her eyes from the trees, as if she were reading them. "France is certainly a land overflowing in virtues," she continued, "perhaps fewer than those attributed to it. However, astuteness is a gift that is as scarce as it is in your land. What've you done in your unpredictable country that caused you to run away like this? Are you a conspirator?"

I knew Margarita and I wouldn't understand each other; nevertheless, I'd always be grateful to her for saving me.

"I'm a magician," I said. "And magic creates misunderstandings."

"I believe it," she said with a smile.

It occurred to me that the discrepancy between her appearance and her voice could've been produced by witchcraft, so I considered my words carefully. With her small arm, she pointed at the bundle on my lap:

"This trip will cost you a few magic tricks."

She didn't leave me an option. Surrounded by the trees' elusive shadows, I untied the satchel's knot and removed the bell jar. It didn't seem to be a magical object, but it was.

Margarita watched, having submitted to my improvised rituals as if I were a great messenger of the extraordinary. Leaning brazenly toward her, I asked her permission and took a small rosebud from her hat. I placed the flower underneath the glass of the bell jar and opened the curtains completely. After a moment the light beams entered and the rose turned pale. Its leaves contracted into flakes, the stem shrunk, the thorns sharpened their tips, and the bud opened. From its center flowed an intense chestnut-brown color that gradually overtook the bright red until it spread to the petals' edges.

"Fabulous," exclaimed my hostess, clapping her hands. "May I touch it?"

Carefully covering up the bell jar, I gently handed her the flower to keep the petals from falling off. She accepted it with equal care, but when she noticed my intention to hide the device, she stopped me:

"Wait. Aren't you going to return my rose to me?"

"That I can't do," I said, tying the satchel's cord. "That's all there is, Margarita. The flower aged in just a few seconds."

"You should know by now," she whispered, "that only one who can bite his own tail can be called a magician. One who can merely change the appearance of things is no more than a scientist's shabby apprentice. The artifact you guard so carefully is simply a time accelerator. There's no difference between this magic trick and the loss of one's virginity. What you travel with is a death machine more offensive than our guillotine. I can just imagine what type of misunderstandings you've had."

She looked at the dried-out rose one more time and placed it back on her hat.

"As you see, I accept what destiny offers me. You may sleep if you prefer and I'll inform you when we cross into France."

# II

My name is Lorenzo Zolo. I was born in Turin, the city of the holy shroud. And maybe because of it, I, like most of the city's inhabitants, possessed a deeply rooted obsession to become well known. I dedicated my time to science or magic, I wasn't too clear about which of the two it was. At that time it was difficult to separate one from the other. Since childhood I'd lived in a room I'd acquired through an uncle, who'd been banished by the family, and his belongings were left in complete neglect when he died. In my mind, inspired by youth, I was also an exile or at least longed to suffer in such a manner. Since my relative had been some sort of inventor, the room consisted of nothing more than the remainders of explosions. Consequently, no one took an interest in his shelter, just as no one had taken an interest in the uncle. I made use of all the instruments I found and added my explosions to the previous ones. Neither the room nor the neighbors seemed to notice the change in tenant. My inventions were nothing more than tricks with gases and I never figured out how to harness those fireworks for some agricultural tool or maritime purpose, which were the only means for me to become a useful member of society.

In the streets there was no shortage of illusionists, but that didn't mean much, because without the magician the invention didn't work, so nobody would buy it. Since the great illusion of Christianity was becoming overshadowed, Christ's name was uttered less and less, and the monks of St. John the Baptist were adding more details to the shroud. Public performances became routine. The people, with the same vehemence with which they resisted believing the illusions, attended the performances to prove there was nothing new under the Italian sky.

As for me, I observed how the inventions succeeded one another and watched their creators get rich and move out of the neighborhood. I knew more than ten people who registered the same spinning gadget. Several times I saw thermometers introduced as a novelty, and yet they merely differed in length from others sold previously. There were other apparatuses that produced some kind of movement, even though people didn't know of what use they'd be. During quite a few years, attempts were made to motivate the unmotivated, as if humanity needed an artificial inspiration and everyone immersed themselves in solving the problem by contributing toys out of a pathetic show of free will. Inventors defended the utter uselessness of their objects, claiming that others in the future would find useful applications for their discoveries. Rumors spread about those who practiced blasphemous experiments in the woods of France; for example, balloons that rose upward with heated air. If I could add here an insensitive element of irony, I'd say that the times were a-changing.

In the plaza one morning, the old man Jacob set up a stand with a glass bell jar that succeeded in ripening food. Since there was no value in aged household items, such as creating rust on a scythe or accelerating a string's loss of elasticity, he used his device to accelerate the aging of fruit. It entered green and came out ripe. When I tried to get closer to compare the taste of his ripened fruit with that of a tree-ripened fruit, the crowd pushed me aside. On a bet, a young rural woman placed her braids in the contraption and won enough money to pay for a few nights at a hostel. When she removed her hair from the bell jar, it was completely gray. At this point in my story, it's important to understand that in those days inventions were common and people wandered from place to place. That afternoon as I returned to my room, my mind obsessed about scarlet fruits and white hair.

All the neighborhoods had more than one genius who spent his time testing out inventions and, above all else, competing with his colleagues. Maybe for that reason Jacob, after a few days, moved his machine to the back of the marketplace. The market vendors, whose fruit wasn't fully ripe, pointed to Jacob's stand, where the customers could finish the process for a fairly low price.

A week later I asked to be the old man's assistant. It was the most ridiculous excuse I'd come up with to get close to the contraption, but all the other ploys had seemed equally laughable. At least this way I could easily disguise my intentions with my natural admiration for wonder. I hoped to discover some kind of hidden pedestal beneath the bell jar that released a certain mixture of gases, similar to those I'd tried, to create the acceleration miracle. I knew the easiest way to show that an object is not magical is to build a similar one.

The old man accepted me. But mind you, he paid me miserably compared to all the fruit he transformed each day. My first job was to walk by the tables and convince the customers not to hesitate to choose unripe fruit, because at the back of the marketplace it could be ripened to the point they wanted. Before long I was running the machine, even though Jacob didn't trust me, and the old man didn't have to leave his chair. It appeared that he enjoyed his invention and having a servant report to him.

"I struggle with you as if you were a domesticated hyena," he confessed one day. "When you're around, not a moment passes when I'm not suspicious of you."

The bell jar perplexed me. It was either pure magic or a very high level of science that didn't involve gases. It required nothing special underneath it, just a piece of wood or a flat surface on which to perform the transformation. If I ruined a fruit, I had to pay for it out of my wages. Consequently, I quickly learned the exact amount of time needed to ripen each fruit. Since I couldn't figure out how to duplicate the invention, I decided to steal it.

Every night I returned home nauseated by the smell of ripe fruit, which never left my nostrils regardless of the numerous fumes lingering in my room from other experiments. I passed the time staring out a little window onto the street and daydreaming about my impending change of fortune. One day Jacob would be careless with his satchel and then he'd never see me again. I'd run away like a common thief. The old man wouldn't look for me much. He'd simply be satisfied in confirming his suspicions about me and consider himself appeased.

To satisfy curiosity about this object, for those who don't believe it or can't imagine it, I'll provide a few details. The bell jar wasn't very thick and could be confused with a circle, since only part of it ever showed from inside the sack. Although its exterior appeared very polished, the inside was covered with finely etched lines that redirected the light, creating the unusual aging process of whatever was inside. The origin of magic objects is always unclear, even more so when, as with this one, it ended up at the back of the marketplace. Jacob claimed that he'd made a living as a metalsmith in Paris. As his clients became fewer, he created this invention and returned to his native land. Within his story there was some truth and some falsehood, as in any story, but without doubt metalworking and exile were two ingredients that guaranteed his memories' authenticity.

It never occurred to me that he might sell the device. Most likely it hadn't crossed his mind either until one afternoon when an incredibly large man with a heavy bag of coins approached us.

"I've come to buy the device," he said.

I looked sideways at the old man's motionless hands. I figured he'd ridicule the man or make some witty reply, but Jacob merely looked withdrawn and skeptical. We'd had little income that day, since few people needed our services in the middle of summer. When the man didn't receive an answer, he tossed the bag of coins onto the table. Jacob lifted it and looked inside without letting me see the sparkle of a single coin. He placed the bell jar in its sack and pulled the drawstring for the last time:

"Take it," he said, and then gave me a victorious look.

With his purchase below his arm, the man walked away, passing the market stands filled with ripe fruit.

"I paid that giant to take your invention away from you," I said, willing my bluff to sound true.

"Follow him," the old man mumbled. "If you really want that thing for yourself, follow him and do what you didn't have the nerve to do to me. In my time, it wasn't so easy for me."

I must've sensed the device was also a curse.

The buyer was staying near the plaza where Jacob had performed his first demonstrations. Maybe, like me, the man had seen those and bided his time until he could collect the money or waited patiently for the old man to become exhausted. I caught up to the giant before he reached the top of the boardinghouse stairs.

"You could use someone who knows how to operate the machine. If you hire me, fewer fruits would be lost in the business."

His height, increased even more by the stairs, made me look like a dwarf. He eyed me closely, probably seeing a boy without a future, who'd just lost his job. Little did he know it wasn't the market that was important to me, but rather the future, which at that moment consisted only of an obsession I'd never let go of, no matter what direction my fate took. In my few moments of good sense, I was ashamed and scolded myself for choosing to live in constant anguish for trying to become well known. Whenever I abandoned my experiments and went to bed early, I couldn't sleep. And every morning as I walked about, I sketched plans and solutions in my mind, which I never actually tried. My behavior showed a callous use of means in pursuit of a single goal, a rise to fame. That confusing sense of shame sustained me and helped me earn a place in heaven, along with a privateer's letter of marque to descend to hell.

"Wait for me in the plaza tomorrow at first light," said the large man. "It's not fruit your device will ripen now, but it's likely you could be useful in making wine."

## III

A vineyard. The giant was taking the bell jar to a grape orchard. I couldn't imagine spending my days far from Turin, destined to the tranquility of farming life. At least he'd identified a more profitable use for the device than ripening fruit. Aging wine could be considered a secure path to wealth.

When I arrived outside the hostel to wait for him, hidden among the columns of the plaza, the sun hadn't yet risen. Later as we walked toward one of the exits, he told me his property was far away, but the walk would be good for us and we'd arrive in good spirits. There was much work awaiting us. I couldn't push aside the idea that in a few moments I'd become an assassin. I'd sacrificed everything. Within a few months, I'd become an insignificant go-between, put up with the traders' jokes and the old man's insults, and when I returned to my room I'd confirm the uselessness of my experiments, which I looked at less and less.

The dagger I'd hidden on my belt poked me while I tried to think of a topic of conversation that'd distract both of us, but I was incapable of clear thoughts.

"It's an incredible thing this invention, don't you think?" my new master asked me.

"Certainly something unexpected," I replied.

"I didn't believe it until I confirmed it myself," he said, kicking the rocks on the path. "My sister fears it, says it's the devil's work."

"She probably has her reasons," I said. At that instant I remember looking at the horizon, it seemed anonymous and irrational. That allegory caused me to think that I was bidding farewell to something great, or that something great was bidding farewell to me.

"However, all objects could be the devil's tool, I think," continued my master. "For example, one day a sickle I have at the house gave me an ugly wound on my leg."

I acted with a lightness that separated me from myself and when I spoke I heard the words as if someone else had spoken them. In those moments, I even separated from my body and saw myself walking alongside the large man, as if I were my own guardian angel. The separation from and return to myself allowed me to accept with indifference the impending criminality of my actions.

"Was the wound very large?" I heard myself ask.

"Enormous," he said. "Here, hold this for me," he said, handing me the satchel.

It'd been so easy to get the bell jar back in my hands. I wouldn't have another chance like this during our whole trip. I saw myself take out the dagger. The giant was bent over to show me the scar. I never found out if he guessed my intentions or simply responded with an instinct of self-preservation. Without hesitation, he stood up and pushed me to the ground, controlling my arm that held the weapon. The satchel with the bell jar got away from me and the base rolled slowly out of my line of vision. I heard it grind, like the groans of a cart crushing the stones on a road, and I swear it was a deafening sound. The wooden base had moved away from me, and I concentrated on not losing sight of the most fragile and fundamental piece. The dagger fell out of my hand when the man squeezed my wrist; however, the desire to acquire an object can convert helplessness into an extraordinary force. I reached for the bell jar, inverted it, and stuck it on top of his head. The sun's rays, which were just beginning to appear, brushed against the glass. Doubled over, he tried to free himself, but the urn remained in place. He started convulsing and wandered off the path like a dazed animal. He fell among the bushes and I could no longer see him.

When I went closer, I saw the bell jar gleaming among the weeds and the farmer's large body nearby, where it'd pushed aside the plants, creating a silhouette. Above his shoulders, the wild plants stood tall, no outline of a head. I picked up the glass without looking at it and moved closer to the body to confirm what had occurred. Between the man's shoulders, where previously there'd been a neck to support the head, there was nothing.

Returning to the path, I picked up the sack and the wooden base. Then, as if the dagger had been the weapon that killed him, rather than the one I held close to my chest, I threw it far away in the direction of Turin before I ran toward the mountains.

# IV

I never imagined the day would come that I'd cross the Alps, to the other side of the world. Emptiness. In my dreams of good fortune, I'd always imagined a more Mediterranean destination. Now, the mountaintops that had fed my childhood fantasies grew larger with each step, like a nightmare returning to collect a debt. I discovered trails that eased my journey as well as that of some woodsmen, but I wasn't a traveler enraptured by the forest's colors and the snow's proximity. I'd transformed myself into an animal more elusive than the beasts of that fabulous landscape. With each step I distanced myself from my homeland.

I slept between the roots of a pine tree and dreamed I was seated at a banquet, where I didn't know anyone, but everyone knew me. I dreamt a brown bear devoured my feet and I didn't even wake up. I dreamt I woke up and there were no animals and I wasn't in the forest.

The roads to France turned out to be more deserted than I thought they'd be. I walked many leagues on the path's edge without having to hide from anyone. When tiredness and uncertainty caused me to stop, I looked up to see a dusty coach approaching very quickly. I stepped out onto the road, as if I were expecting the carriage's arrival. I feared a furtive gunshot, not because it would kill me, but because it would break the bell jar into pieces. Luckily the coachman, possibly more frightened than I was, stopped the carriage. The horses' front hooves descended around me, as they shook their halters and whinnied. It was a small coach, a perfect miniature that could only belong to the neighboring land, and it would take me there.

# V

I rested with my arms securely around the death machine, as Margarita had called it, until she woke me:

"Magician! Magician!"

The coach came to a stop on a wooden bridge.

"To the right, following the creek, you'll come across a village where you can take refuge and earn a living with your apparatus. Get rich quickly and then sell it. With the money you earn, you'll be able to start a new life in Paris as a gardener, metalworker, or whatever you find, because all of France is troubled these days. Listen to my advice and don't let yourself be deceived by dreams of grandeur."

"What's the name of the village?" I asked.

"Adjani. It's a quirky, but beautiful town."

I got out of the carriage at the bridge as if I were entering a painting or a dream.

"Thank you, Margarita. May I look for you when I get to Paris?"

"Oh, I'm not going so far, my friend. You can look for me in Lyon, but you won't find me. I'm an insect."

I saw her relax back in her seat, with her childish face lost behind the window and the dried rose still on the side of her hat. I tried to memorize the coat of arms on the door, but then remembered many coaches used the same shield to hide the identity of the passengers. So, I forgot the images. I never went to Lyon.

# VI

The zigzag path, guarded by two rows of trees with few leaves, seemed to delay my arrival more than guide me to the town. I didn't notice any differences between this place and the villages back home. The path ended between two dilapidated houses, making me wonder how I might make a fortune in such a place. Some children ran about in circles, but didn't pay any attention to me. They simply continued their game, at one point running around me as if I were just another tree. Amid their shouts of "Arrête-toi! . . . Stop!" I understood my limited ability to introduce myself without being able to speak the language. Margarita had been unique. Here my words wouldn't help me much in this new situation. It occurred to me then that the coach ride had been more of a practice opportunity for my hostess than for me, as her last chance to use her Italian.

When I arrived in the center of Adjani, I realized why it was the perfect place to make a fortune. The entire settlement was a marketplace. The inhabitants, for the most part visitors from large cities, stayed for many days in questionable, wooden inns. Rich and poor alike intermingled there, all admirers of magic. It was a naïve and hysterical mass of people, who craved fantasy and illusions. There wasn't any gambling and no one got rich from the performances, except the conjurers themselves. I'd definitely arrived in France.

From a corner I saw a giant shoe appear. A wooden doll, as large as a tree, slowly walked forward while its head turned from side to side. The fleet of puppeteers hanging from its shoulders, waist, and neck propelled life into the doll, aided by wheels and pulleys. Groups on the ground chased the doll, pretending it was about to step on them, and many dared to cross the shadow of its feet. At the risk of sounding inappropriate, I'd say that it came close to a Royal de Luxe performance, similar to the one they did for the twentieth anniversary of the Berlin Wall's fall, for example.

Watching that spectacle was akin to feeling the world really was approaching its end and there was nothing left to do but recycle the same surprises. I saw fire-eaters, fire-breathers, fortune-tellers, beheadings (that I didn't want to see), levitations, throwing knives, machines, and mimes. I saw my childish enthusiasm and my adolescent boredom. The people moved from one magician to another, mouths agape like bubbles bursting in a boiling broth. I could still see the doll's body walking away down other streets. Its smiling face keeping an eye on the crowds, first to one side and then the other. During the excitement on the street, I ended up in the front row of a performance. At this moment everyone wanted to participate in the tricks of an acknowledged magician, who made a chick appear on the palm of his hand, moved it in front of the open-mouthed faces, and then made the chick disappear. I waited for the point when he'd come close to me with the bird in his open hand. The illusionist turned very slowly, or maybe I perceived that everything moved slowly, almost stopping. As if in another time dimension. My opponent spun around on one leg, like a music box figure. On his hand the small bird retreated from the shouts, while the wind and acceleration of the circle it traversed ruffled its soft feathers. I waited, already having prepared the bell jar. I saw it approaching, little by little, held in an imaginary orbit, until it was in front of me. I exchanged glances with the magician, who was preparing to make the bird disappear again. At that moment I snatched the bird, trapped it under the glass, and raised it above the slighted and amazed crowd that took a step back to allow me more space. Inside the glass, the bird grew, acquiring more colors and contorting into a puzzling form. Then when I removed the glass, at the exact moment that it was a splendid specimen of a rooster, he let out a resounding cock-a-doodle-doo, causing people to stop and turn toward me in amazement. I expected retaliation from the other conjurer, owner of what previously had been a chick; however, he was so moved by the miracle that tears ran down his face. I offered him the rooster and he hugged it as if it were a valuable treasure. It seemed to me that even the giant puppet, at a distance, turned quietly and smiled, welcoming me to Adjani.

I ran through the galleries robbing fruit from the vendors and giving the ripened fruit to the people who followed me, falling over themselves. In the last doorway, an old woman watched me from her window. I presented her with a bouquet of herbs that I'd just made bloom and without losing sight of the partially opened door, I entered her house, leaving the multitudes in the street demanding I come outside again.

# VII

Claire was no taller than my navel. Her straight, dirty hair fell around her shoulders like a cape, and she moved assertively, with solid footsteps echoing on the floor. After obtaining the bell jar, I figured all that was left for me was a supernatural encounter. Claire approached me, speaking with a mixture of affection and conspiracy that wasn't difficult to interpret. With the intention of starting my new life in hiding, I made hand signals to her so she'd believe her guest magician was mute.

Her house extended along a hallway, both sides full of cages with colorful birds that screeched and reeked of wood rotted by their filth. Claire led me between the cages to the patio, while she lulled the birds to sleep in an indistinguishable French that was simultaneously bawdy and maternal. I stayed inside the remainder of the day, resting in a dusty room. Once in a while I could hear Claire shooing away the curious people who'd approached her window. The birds conspired with her to enhance her fussing. My plan was to allow time to increase the people's curiosity and with any luck obtain a go-between. Despite my hand signals, I suspected Claire had seen in me a desperate foreigner, who took refuge in the behaviors of a deaf-mute.

Quite aware of my failure with aging the rose during my trip, I told myself such a trick would be a repulsive act for the

French. In my country the magic trick would've brought much applause and a sense of victory. Or perhaps not. Resting my face upon a battered, sinking bed, I decided to create a type of show that bestowed life, not decay, similar to the successful spectacle with the rooster or replication of the fruit-ripening trick.

Nighttime in Adjani was cool and fresh. The people gathered in bars or ate meat kabobs sold on the streets. If a vendor let a spark escape that raised suspicions about some fantastic trick, people considered him a clumsy fool. The village appeared smaller at night. The houses, most of which were no more than three stories, shared their roofs, pressing up against each other. The sky gave off an intense blue that seemed French or ocean-like. I counted few stars. Chewing on a beef kabob, I wandered around without anyone recognizing me.

The next day the townspeople looked for me. The same illusionists that'd been set aside the day before joined the throngs that Claire easily dealt with. I climbed up through the patio and waited on a roof behind them. At my signal Claire pointed at me. I'd taken a few eggs from my landlady and placed them in the bell jar, holding it for everyone to see until I removed the colorful birds that took flight and flew around, bewildered by the crowd's shouts and raised hands. In my silence I discovered a talent for mime I'd never explored. Above the roofs, I became a master of gestures and acrobatics, earning applause and unveiling incredible birds, even in groups of three or five. At the end of a performance, I requested fruits and ripened them before tossing them to the crowd. These made me remember my innocent life in Turin, when I was full of dreams. While I moved toward Claire's roof, I continued my act and then with a bow dropped into her patio, as my protector closed the windows.

I forgot Margarita's advice and settled into my new life in Adjani. After the birds, I matured wines that I poured into the bell jar as if it were a bowl and then sprinkled on my fans. I forced rosebuds to bloom and aged cheeses Claire had obtained the night before. The cheese slices I presented to the crowd caused a fracas. One morning someone in the crowd shouted: "*Bravo!*" and the sound of Italian almost caused me to drop the glass. In the first row stood a young woman who looked like she was from Piedmont. She applauded with an enthusiasm I hadn't seen before. She was wearing a colorful scarf on her head and a tattered dress that caressed her body's curves. I jumped down to Claire's patio without finishing the show. I waited until my landlady, who was surprised by my act's brevity, sent the onlookers away.

I peeked through the crack in the window, looking for the young woman's silhouette. The crowd had dispersed and continued its usual routine of knife-throwing and sword-swallowing. I decided to look for her. Because of my height and not appearing as a magician on a roof, I figured I could move easily among the crowd without being recognized, just like at night. When I turned toward the door, Claire was waiting for me with the bell jar wrapped in its satchel. Perhaps she'd seen everything, or maybe the unfinished performance coupled with my spying through the crack caused her to suspect imminent danger. The birds I'd made hatch had returned to her patio, drawn by the others, thus doubling her brood. That, more so than the coins people had tossed to her, was my payment to her.

I took the object and spoke for the first time. I wanted to be honest with her and, even if she didn't understand a single word, I owed it to her:

"My name is Lorenzo Zolo," I told her. "I was born in Turin, the city that protects the sacred shroud. I don't know if you're telling me my time to go has come or if you simply don't dare to be alone with this thing. Thank you for everything."

"It isn't the first time in my reckless life I've crossed paths with this bell jar," she said in a rough but recognizable Italian. "Good luck."

She took a few slow steps and opened the door for me. The colorful birds screeched, annoyed by the light from the plaza. Claire quieted them with a short yell, then closed the door without looking at me.

# VIII

I walked through the whole town, but didn't find her. I came across many idlers without them recognizing me as one of their own. I ended up on a street where they'd stretched out the colossal marionette, leaving little room to walk around with its body taking up almost the entire width of the lane. So close up, it was difficult to recognize its parts. Its head rested to one side with the eyes closed. The wooden lips, parted, still smiled at me. I walked to its side and stroked one of its fingers.

When night fell I decided to seek refuge in a tavern. There someone grabbed me by the arm:

"In an open area in the woods, I have a bottle of wine from your country, *paisano*."

Her words returned me to the Turin I'd fled, and the vision of the meeting made me tremble. She moved ahead of me and I followed, my eyes fixed on her scarf that fell around her neck and stuck to the sweat on her back. She was dressed like the most frugal of rural girls and walked with a lightness in her step. It was obvious as she walked through the streets of that marvel-filled city that she competed with Adjani in beauty and she thought them daft for not understanding the natural process of death. Once in a while she turned around and beckoned me. An ancient and distant force drew me to her, as if to a siren. I wanted to speak to her, but I didn't trust my voice after the long silence I'd recently broken. The bell jar was heavy and became uncomfortable to carry. We left the town on the same road by which I'd arrived, possibly the only way to get to that part of the world.

A horse tied to a tree stopped rooting the ground and raised its head when we arrived, then returned to chewing the grass. If this woman had ended up in Adjani, I thought to myself, she must've made a mistake similar to mine. We were in the heart of the forest in the middle of the night. Leaned up against the wagon she said was her home, I bit the tip of her chin, then licked her neck and shoulder. I heard my breathing in the space between her breasts as they pressed up against me. I was a fugitive and accepted my situation. Taking a step back, she led me to where she'd prepared a campfire. There she turned to talk to me, her Italian vibrating like a spell.

"It took me a long time to find this lost town," she said, taking a bottle out of the wagon and serving me a cup. "Do some magic for me. Make this wine rancid."

In the light of the fire, I found my bell jar and held out the base, where she set the glass. She asked me to age the wine one hundred years. I moved the device closer to the flames.

"It's ready," I announced. "Drink a one-hundred-year-old wine."

She tried it without admiring the flavor.

"I'm going to show you," she said, "the remains of a magic trick that brought me here. Rest there against that tree."

She attempted to dance a pleasant dance and then untied the scarf from her hair. At first I thought it was the wine, the fire, or the oceanic French night of Adjani that disfigured her hair. If she'd had serpents for hair, it wouldn't have scared me as much as this. Her long hair lost its chestnut color at her shoulders and from there down it was as white as bone. Her braided hair, one afternoon in a Turin plaza, had experienced more than the effects of my bell jar. An object of the devil. I tried to approach her when she pulled the rope that lay on the ground and yelled:

"Now, brother!"

From behind the tree where I'd been resting appeared the headless giant with his right wrist tied to the rope. He squeezed me between his arms, which were even stronger now that he was a monstrous creature. The girl threw herself on top of me and snatched the bell jar out of my hands.

"Hold him tightly!"

She took out a torch and lit it in the fire. Raising the jar without its base, she pressed it against my abdomen while she brought the torch closer for more light. My body writhed. I howled like an insect thrown in a fire. The giant held me with so much strength that the pain inflicted by his grip competed with the burning of my stomach. The girl brought the glass close to all parts of my body, as if she were trying to catch a small critter, like a slippery rat, that was running all over me, fleeing from the apparatus. My body began to decompose in circular pieces that fell to the ground, rotted. I came apart, leaving only tendons, droopy wrinkles, and bones transformed to dust. I became sand. Each time I resisted less, since with every moment there was less and less of me. I possessed no control or will over my wasted body. If I weren't telling of such a dramatic moment in my life, I'd add it was like listening to Slipknot in the front row of a concert playing "All Hope is Gone."

"Here, brother," I heard my captor say. "Here's the bloody man's head."

With one hand the giant took the bell jar and with his other he held me by my hair. His clumsiness surprised me; he wouldn't have been any good at aging wine, I thought. The last thing I saw was the girl's white hair move through the air as the forest disappeared. As the bell jar consumed my head, it fell out of the giant's hands and broke on the ground against a tree root.

I begged that my soul would rise like those rebels in their balloons filled with hot air, but alas I remained among the leaves and roots. The fire died. The next day in that place there was nothing more than a broken, useless bell jar filled with dry leaves scattered by the winds, without being consumed by it. To one side lay my right hand that, by a mere oversight, had escaped the deadly aging process.

# IX

I imagine the same children who on the day of my arrival had run among the hills of Adjani picked me up from the ground and were not surprised. They'll be children of a disillusioned generation. I can picture them in a circle around my hand, which will remind them of an amazing insect. Perhaps they took a moment to recognize it for what it truly was, then one of them suggested placing a pen in my hand and some paper nearby so I could write. Maybe they believe I can predict the future, but that's just my own vanity. What could some children running through the trees want to find in the future? They probably gave me the instruments, because an unconnected hand can't do anything else but write and these words will be, without doubt, a revelation of the absent body.

My would-be lover with two-toned hair and the monster led by a rope must've fled in their wagon, their hands empty. In my current state any plan of vengeance is absurd. On the other hand, I still maintain the same feeling of wholeness with which I used to create explosions in my room by the market plaza. Only now my remaining piece embarrasses me and holds me back. I don't know how much longer I'll live, nor under what circumstances.

Now that I no longer am and yet still exist, I'm able to admire everything with a clarity that simultaneously includes me but does not involve me. I carry with me very strong, clairvoyant memories, which I most likely won't be able to write down. I even remember things that never happened, because possibly they're about to happen. My life is an infinite line. In the future, a poet will write "Ode to Niagara." Don't ask me what that word means. I don't know. It's probably another splendid monster. In the future, there'll be stories of authenticity. There'll be stories. I complete this text that is written from scratch and whose pages' order I can't guarantee. I believe I'm writing. I believe I feel the pen between my fingers. Undoubtedly it's still July of the year that it was, one thousand seven hundred eighty-nine. Now that I consider it in this way, I'm content to die like this, to disappear. After having confirmed the warmth of our days, I predict that this, and no other, is the true end of time.

\*

Toward the end of the year, I found work in a London window factory. A cutting machine traced fine lines on a sheet of glass, which then broke with a slight upward movement. In this way they created rectangles and later fit them with frames. If one of the pieces didn't break properly or a corner was ruined, I'd dispatch the glass pane to another machine that sent it back to the process's beginning as raw material. That was my job while I looked for a clue to the whereabouts of the Third Library.

While walking around adjacent areas of the factory, I learned glass in fact comes from sand, which reminded me of the old, sand hourglasses and their role in representing time. Sand trickling down from one globe to another. I perceived the glass of a door, a bar, and a shop window with motionless mannequins as if it were frozen in time. The majority of the factory workers were immigrants, far from their families. To me, it seemed such an indifference of destiny and of my imagination that we worked to stop time. We stretched and polished lakes of glass that reflected the world with more brilliance than the original and at night when we turned on a light in a room the glass reflected our loneliness. Without intending to do so, I began to create a misguided moment of rebellion, my left hand's minute blunder ruined the corner's right angle and thus the whole piece. So, I took it to the other machine and let it fall into the void, stopping time and initiating the cycle that contributes to the ongoing illusion that days go by and, in some moment, my journey would continue. Inherent to temporary jobs is an imaginary potential that comes very close to irreverence.

"Years ago while I was convalescing in a Lisbon clinic," one of the workers said during a break, "I shared the room with another patient and every morning they brought us two different newspapers, which were always out-of-date. Although we didn't like to read and were too lazy to translate the Portuguese, we were always bored, so each of us took a newspaper and later told the other what we'd read. We competed to find the best story and, in our determination to win, it wasn't long before one of us made up the first lie. Later, we hid behind the pages for a few minutes and then began to relate some terrible news story. Curiously, one time we invented a story that appeared a few days later as an actual event in one of the outdated newspapers."

We were sitting in a semi-circle and eating turkey sandwiches that made us a little sleepy. It was getting dark and the formidable Tate Modern building was visible on the other side of the Thames, like a ship docked in a gloomy city. In the distance the London Eye watched, in homage to all the Eiffel Tower's problems.

Someone else told of a city where he was going to live, in which everyone saw each other at least twice a day.

"Nevertheless, it's true," said the man choking on a piece of bread, "that a neighborhood or city exists in southern Florida, where visitors always encounter each other two times a day, without fail. They attribute this fascinating coincidence to the Tropic of Cancer's proximity to the place. Nonetheless due to the definition of meetings, rules haven't been recognized that verify what exactly constitutes an encounter between two people, nor how the repetitions are produced. As such, O City could imitate a common, ordinary city or suburb.

"A hit man follows his victim to O City. So as not to mistake his target's face, he takes out a photo of the man and studies it for the last time. Just as the doors to an elevator are closing, he stumbles upon his quarry. They exchange a brief look. Then the assassin quickly runs up the stairs and arrives at the floor above before the elevator arrives, but when the doors open it's empty. Since the photo had been taken in O City, the killer's glance at it constituted the first encounter.

("A hit man memorizes the victim's face outside of O City. When he thinks he can recognize him easily, he travels to the city. He finds and shoots him. Before dying, the man says: it's impossible for you to kill me, we have to conclude our second encounter. The assassin walks away. Then, at a distance, he takes out of his pocket the dead man's photo, which was taken in O City. He looks at it for the last time and tosses it into the gutter.)

"One morning a tourist lost her six-year-old daughter in O City. An official tried to calm her down, assuring her cases like these were easily solved. He ushered her into the nearest shop and told the owner the woman had lost her little girl. He warned the woman that if she had a photo of the girl not to take it out, nor show it to anyone, to be on the safe side. The place was a hat store. The tourist was taken to a room where some women sewed the cloth pieces. There she kept busy watching the work and even helped to make one of the samples. The policeman returned later when the workers were getting ready to leave for the day. The woman asked about her daughter and he said she should wait a little longer. When the afternoon was almost over, the door opened and the girl walked in.

"Shortly before midnight a fugitive from justice enters a motel in the outskirts of O City. A young employee welcomes her and leads her to her room. Later, while the girl is taking a shower, the young man, dressed like his dead mother, enters the bathroom with a knife, and kills her.

"In the morning, a thief sneaks into a house in O City and gets as far as the main bedroom, where the woman keeps her jewelry. If he is unfortunate, she awakes and surprises him while he's filling his bag, and the thief will hit her hard enough to knock her unconscious. Later, he picks her up, puts her on the bed, and fans her. He waits until she recovers and after she sees him again, he escapes permanently.

"In O City when a magician makes a young woman from the audience disappear, she's not obliged by the theatrical performance to reappear minutes later on the podium. Each of the spectators will have the opportunity to encounter her again that same night on the sidewalk or eating an ice cream behind a store window."

When I'd finished my sandwich, I imagined that O City's public library, if it had one, would be made of mirrors and the books would be unlimited. Their stories would have a single protagonist with multiple, brilliant perspectives. Upon visiting it, I wouldn't know if my conversation had been with the Librarian or with one of his images. His suspicion would be in my favor, since he wouldn't know if he'd spoken with me or not.

On a park bench, a homeless man was repairing a world map he'd drawn himself with the precision of the first mapmakers. He continuously murmured:

*In a forest, in a volcano, in a wave, in a dune*
*In a beautiful day in Slovenia*
*In the autumn*
*In a tulip field*
*In the cool waters in Oregon*
*In the mystical clouds of New Zealand*
*In the road less traveled*
*In a morning mist in Havana*
*In a forest, in a volcano, in a wave, in a dune . . .*

In the splendid galleries of a Russian subway, I managed to stumble upon the Third Library. The entrance, protected by a legless man, was concealed by a broken shelf full of old, hardcover books that resembled State Hermitage Museum catalogs, fashion magazines, and maps of St. Petersburg. Everything had exorbitant prices, as if I'd walked into a GUM department store. The Librarian of the Third Library was burning incense in an ornate candlestick holder and reading the smoke spirals. A few meters from him, an adolescent and his mother waited, peering down the empty tunnel.

The train stopped and dozens of passengers got off, moving between the Librarian and me. The woman and youth threw themselves into the crowd to get onto the train before the doors closed, thus causing them to miss their chance to board. As the noise of the machine and the murmur of the pedestrians faded away, the white light from the dome above flickered and the man said to me:

"In October 1876, our Fyodor Dostoyevsky wrote an article published in *A Writer's Diary*, in which he commented on an event in the courts. A young, pregnant woman was punished with two years of forced labor and exile in Siberia for the rest of her life. She was condemned for the attempted murder of her six-year-old stepdaughter, whom she'd pushed out a window. The woman had been tormented by her husband's constant criticisms and comparisons to his previous wife. After the incident, Katerina refused to look at the scene of the girl on the ground, but instead walked, most likely with soft steps to cushion the weight of her abdomen, to the police station to confess. The girl, however, didn't die. People said she was in good health, which we understand to mean she suffered no physical harm. Dostoyevsky defends Katerina by attributing certain 'extraordinary manifestations' to her pregnant state. According to him, no one can deny that an expecting mother, especially during her first pregnancy, tends to be exposed to certain influences and strange feelings that impact her spirit in unusual ways. From this explanation, he begins to create a defense of Katerina based on the key principle that it's preferable to err on the side of clemency than severity. With each line, our author finds himself identifying more and more with the conflict he argues. In the end he's committed to his literary overflow and proposes scenes of the family's future, in which once the baby is born, Katerina is obliged to leave forever. Dostoyevsky presents us with a person motivated by a labyrinth-like awareness. Without realizing the characters' emergence, we witness a couple who become aware of the love that had always existed between them, but was sadly discovered at the moment she's imprisoned. They even talk about the cold in Siberia and the warm boots for the trip. The six-year-old girl clings to her stepmother and cries about the strange set of circumstances that established them as enemies and now vexes their family's harmony. She'll take food to her lonely mother:

"'For you, mother. Father sent you tea and sugar. Tomorrow he'll come to see you.'

"We watch the goodbyes take place on the sidewalk, where the newborn, held in his father's arms, lets out a feeble cry as the train begins its journey and the mother's image slips away into the distance. Dostoyevsky finishes by asking for a little reflection about the sentence's crudeness, having himself also endured several years of exile in a place similar to where Katerina will end up. Until this point one can admire the story. A few months later in the December edition of *A Writer's Diary*, the embarrassed author reflected on how a novelist can start from a common event, so uninspiring it could actually be real, and result in the process allowing his pen to run wild and predict a family's future, thus converting them into characters of a daring narrative. But it doesn't conclude there. Motivated by the empathy he experienced with his characters, Dostoyevsky risked visiting Katerina. We can imagine devious methods and bribes in the prison underworld, even if there were none. Upon seeing her, Dostoyevsky recognized her as his Katerina, and there embracing her was her remorseful, tearful husband. The girl wasn't there, because she was in school. The writer had only mistaken the warm boots for the trip, the tea with sugar, and the sex of the baby; it was another girl."

"The center is unmoving, but miniscule," I replied. "Russia is such a vast land it's impossible to move away from it without being close to it."

"Everything vanishes, but also endures," said the Librarian, wrapping his finger around a rising column of smoke. "Of the literary figures these many years, three disturb me more than the weight of my torso: the collector, the voyeur, and the sniper. All three are obsessive figures, but the degree of obsession varies from one to the other. The first reclaims a space with himself at the center, establishing another reality in which he prefers to entrench himself in a system that offers him consistency and time. He creates his own circular history. The second, thirsty for stories, is an insatiable, famished character, who watches reality from above with the condition that reality doesn't notice his gaze. He disfigures his own existence so the world he wants to admire actually exists, no matter what. The third is a particle in the air. He puts his eye to the conflict's vortex and disarms it or causes it; nevertheless, he is honestly disinterested. He is a nihilistic narrator, who motivates history and then abandons it, leaving it to just happen while he caresses his money."

"When Hemingway mentions one-eighth of the iceberg," I said, "he assumes the existence of a totality, but if the eighth becomes a suggestion, the totality is essentially a convention of history, since all fictional material is enormous. There's no iceberg. I simply don't accept the iceberg."

"That's fine, you may spend as much time as you want inside; however, when you depart, you must leave a book," added the man, as he leaned toward a ring of gray smoke.

# Book III: The Book of Perfection
# Apropos of the Wet Snow

# A

Perfection is hypnotic.

Such a statement seems to be confirmed in an ambiguous passage of a Dostoyevsky novel. In it he recounts how Vasili decides to shoot a waiter merely because from his apartment window a few stories up, he could see, through a missing roof section of the tavern across the street, the vodka server's torso that rarely moved.

Being so perfect, the deed is unexpected. According to the story, after feeling tempted by this suggestion of geometric fate, Vasili visits the tavern one night. He searches the waiter's face for some type of annoyance or vexation to justify the unsteadiness Vasili had experienced from his room's high window. While there he meets Sonia, a prostitute who accompanies him the entire night, and our hero ends up proposing to her. She follows him to his room, where they attempt sex, but fail due to his lack of energy. Sonia steals the notes for a novel she finds on the table and leaves two ruble coins in exchange. It's almost sunrise when Vasili awakes, discovers the coins, realizes his papers are missing, walks over to the window with the rifle, and shoots the waiter.

This passage is introduced in a conversation between two characters in a cheap restaurant, which isn't the same tavern in the story. The author's withdrawal from the story at this point and the two men's certainty about Vasili's fate imply he wasn't charged with anything. The micro-story's conclusion suggests that someone wouldn't accept punishment if the only identified motive were perfectionist hypnosis. And yet, if an event isn't written into the narrative that supports it, does it stop being an event of interest and is it thus relegated to a place far from the narrative canon?

Following this train of thought, one could fully agree to consider a reading based on the human condition. The ideals of justice, compassion, destiny, and God would be permitted by certain awareness of the Story. The Reader, who'd become the person sitting at the table next to the two men drinking and talking loudly, will ask himself while turning his drinking glass: how are the actual occurrences received through a narrative and how, in turn, are the other incidents that don't fulfill the established logic or plot excluded? On the contrary, how is it that some literature is marginalized because it doesn't fit the same molds that've been used to represent life, even by that same literature? And perfection and its hypnosis, where do they fit in, as one or the other?

The man at the next table will also believe Vasili's motive to be very clear: his novel was stolen. He was robbed for the ridiculous price of two rubles, which doesn't even pay for the paper it was written on, and he wasn't allowed a second chance in the morning to prove his virility. Everyone would've shot the waiter.

But no. It's literature that's almost worth two rubles. Vasili had studied point B, who isn't a waiter, nor a human being who could annoy him. He's simply a seductive point hidden behind a chance barrier. Vasili attempted to humanize him, hoping to alter that inertia, trying to find out if he liked him or not, and in doing so encountered Sonia; then again, the prostitute isn't the motive either. She came to conduct business and ended up converting him, who was formerly Vasili, into point A, without a novel, without a future wife or kids, without anything.

Upon hearing this story, and especially if you're in the lands of the subsequent Anton Chekhov, the first thing that'd make the Reader doubt this story could be the appearance of the rifle, but in essence the rifle itself isn't the most dubious issue of the story. We can soothe the literary convention with the following illustration:

It's true that when occupying cheap rooms, one tends to find forgotten remnants from the previous tenant. Wrinkled papers, a glove with holes, or even a locked suitcase, which when the tenant is unable to open it, is used as a chair, table, or stool to climb on to check the wardrobe tops for other discoveries. Vasili found the rifle. Correct?

Hidden beneath the mattress, it made him uncomfortable the first two nights and he thought it was a wooden slat that'd slipped out of place. He reckoned he'd take some time making a few adjustments. While looking for the board, he lifted the mattress and found the rifle. What had been considered an uncomfortable wooden slat during several years now turned out to be a rifle. Vasili remembered his father taking him hunting for hares with his white dog when he was a boy. In the quiet of the room with its one window, he imagined he heard gunshots and his father's joyful shouts. He lifted the rifle to his shoulder, placed a hand on the belly of the cold wood, and grazed the trigger with the other hand. Wondering about the sight's accuracy, he pointed the rifle arbitrarily out the window. In the sight's center, peering through a hole in the roof of the tavern across the street, he saw the body of a waiter, who slowly poured a tall drink of vodka. Instead of pulling the trigger, he made a sound with his mouth, pow! From the moment he discovered the rifle under the mattress, Vasili sensed it was loaded.

So, there you have the rifle, window, and introduction of a perfect crime. What could be missing?

From the window he contemplated the rooftops of St. Petersburg. On the sidewalk below, a prostitute walked by. Clearly she shivered from the cold. Vasili felt a certain type of pity for the woman behind the prostitute. Never one to enjoy the sympathy of her warm breasts, it's needless to say she didn't matter to him. His pity was more aligned with "sociology." Pity because a man from a window high up in the opposite building knew she was a prostitute merely by looking at her.

Grabbing pen and paper, he began to write a passionate letter.

*Miss* ____, he left a blank space:

*Seeing you from my window, I have wondered: what awaits this woman?* It's too much to add that he wouldn't have the honesty to scribble: since I saw you jumping from here to there like a hungry finch, I told myself that, yes, she is a whore. *What awaits this woman? I ask myself. Something from within brought me the answer. This woman waits for you. She strolls below your window with nervous, sharp steps. I have decided to write a letter to this woman. And I should deliver it to her personally and wait for her to read it. She may possibly forget about the cold wind of St. Petersburg, look at me, and tell me thank you. And later, softly, as only women know how to do, she'll tell me she prefers the blizzard of the street because, I shouldn't be mistaken in any way, she knows it better than she knows me.*

After folding it with careless geometry, he placed the letter in his pocket. He hid the rifle again under the mattress and went down the stairs two by two, disturbing the other tenants.

"This letter is for you."

Sonia looked at him, opened her small eyes wide, and moved to one side, the door to the tavern visible behind her: "For me?"

If Sonia had known she was nothing more than a sentimental figure in the scene Vasili had invented to get closer to a table in order to develop some type of connection with the vodka server, she would've accepted anyhow. Of course Vasili knew the deference of the finch, but preferred to confuse the proximity to the seduction point with some story that'd justify his presence and, at the same time, disguise his investigation. He chose a table where he could watch the waiter constantly, as he served each drink. However, Sonia stopped him before he could sit down.

"Please," she said, "allow me to sit here. I don't like the view from the window."

That's how Vasili spent the whole night with his back to point B. He observed the abstract scenery of the glass window in which Sonia's body was silhouetted as her bird-like eyes swayed in the neurotic calligraphy.

"What's your name?"

"Sonia."

He dipped his pen in the pot of dark tea where she warmed her hands. He wrote the name in the empty space on the letter and returned it to her.

"Once there was a time when they wrote me many letters," she commented. "One was named Danilov. He was an assassin, who'd killed half the world and yet he wrote to me. I don't know where all those papers ended up . . ."

"One never knows where letters will wind up," said Vasili.

"It's true. You never know." She folded the page, which easily surrendered its previous folds, and stuck it in her bodice. "For me, letters are good."

Vasili was pleased by that simple proclamation.

"For me as well," he said. Of course, with those words he merely intended to convey he liked what he'd heard.

Sonia said writing letters seemed very sweet. He assumed she'd meant to say tender. What Danilov had written in his letters might've made him seem a good person in others' eyes.

"For me," she said, and at this point in the story Vasili already realized Sonia liked to repeat those two words, "in letters you write the truth. If you don't say things as you would in another moment, it's because in letters you want to be closer to the truth. The rest is pure fiction."

Vasili swallowed his vodka and contemplated Sonia's image with the glass-window background. Not surprised by her use of the word fiction, he pondered where he'd place fiction and where he'd place the truth she talked about. He reasoned that even though the motive of his invitation was to find a pretext for shooting the waiter, the letter in which he wrote about the prostitute waiting for him wasn't entirely fictitious. Sonia, in essence, was waiting for him, because he was at that time a man just like any other. While she played with her glass, the color returning to her hands, he drank too much in hopes his vodka server would irritate him in some way and, if he were lucky, would toss him out into the cold street.

Meanwhile, Sonia talked about old letters, St. Petersburg in the middle of the night, and what a good man the assassin was who used to write to her. Sonia, of course, was talking to herself out of loneliness.

"Miss Sonia," he'd written her name with tea, "will you marry me?"

Here the Reader will want to interrupt the men's conversation and repeat that Vasili is fleeing the crime, from the perfectionist hypnosis of segment AB, and settling into a life in St. Petersburg. He'll marry Sonia and abandon his queasiness, fascination, and even his anti-literary destiny. Vasili appears to desperately want to insert himself in history. However, by managing to accept something the two men hadn't mentioned, the Reader will doubt himself just before standing up and interrupting their discussion. His anti-history is related in order to avoid a predictable narrative. The Reader sits down again and listens.

They went up the stairs slowly, at a melancholy tempo, allowing a few laughs to escape their lips. Sonia covered her mouth with both hands to avoid waking the tenants and he held his arms open wide, bracing himself clumsily against the walls. There'll be a day when they remember this moment like an old, grainy record with limited light. Sonia's skirt was floating above the stairs in light and dark contrasts, like an enormous, disoriented butterfly in a narrow scene, as Vasili grabbed her from behind, smiling and unstable from the vodka.

They opened the door hurriedly, pretending to invade a stranger's room, and slammed the door behind them. Vasili fell heavily on the bed. Sonia looked around the place.

"What a lot of books you have!" she laughed, as if she'd discovered something supernatural.

Vasili didn't know how to respond.

"They say books corrupt men. Do you like books a lot?"

A mumble coming through the wall from the room next door interrupted them. Both became quiet and pushed themselves against the wall.

"I like them," whispered Vasili, moving closer to Sonia's face, as she pressed her ear to the wall. "To tell you the truth, I like them a lot."

He started to laugh heartily and Sonia signaled that they should be quiet so they could hear what was being said on the other side of the wall.

"He's a mystic," Vasili told her from where he sat on the floor. "He spends the entire day praying. Climb up on the bed and you can see him through a hole."

Sonia climbed the stairs, taking care not to make noise, and looked through the hole. Vasili lay down on the floor and looked under the prostitute's skirt.

"He's an old man, with a frightening beard. He's kneeling before an icon and prays with his eyes closed." She sat down on the bed as if she wanted to forget what she'd just seen. "The old mystic makes me sad. Come on, let's make love."

She complained about an out-of-place wooden slat under the mattress and moved to one side. Since Vasili was slow to remove his clothes and she still didn't feel anything hard except for the wooden slat she was moving away from, she stood up ready to surrender the innocence of her lips to her future husband's private parts.

"Can you sing a song for me to block out the prayers?" she asked the distracted Vasili.

He hummed an old Tartary song, amid laughter that mixed with the old neighbor's murmurings and Sonia's labored breathing. He sang until he fell asleep, a few moments later.

His future wife stopped her efforts, which had produced limited results, and returned to looking through the peephole. The old man didn't seem to have moved since the last time she spied on him. At this juncture, she stopped stalking the mystic and assessed her own situation. She was curious about the old man's manic dogma. At her feet lay a man with delusions of being a perfectionist, who'd proposed to be her husband and surround her with books, something she'd never wanted.

She got off the bed, pulled the sheet over Vasili's legs to hide the sight of his flaccid penis, walked over to the window, and looked out over all of St. Petersburg. It was snowing. She wanted to take a few books with her to burn later on a little street near the pier to warm herself and forget the night she'd just spent. She took everything out of her pockets, two coins of one ruble each and left them on the table to pay for the stolen goods. Then she noticed a bundle of pages with writing and assumed she'd do less damage if she took them rather than one of the bound books. She hid the packet of papers beneath her clothing and walked down the stairs after carefully closing the door behind her.

"What could Sonia have felt when she saw all of St. Petersburg?" wondered the Reader at his table, with the risk of losing the thread of conversation between the two men. Perhaps she felt the same way she did as she took each paper out of her skirt and threw it onto the fire to warm herself in the early morning of the faithless. Or possibly, the men would suggest, she heard Vasili's voice humming the Tartary song.

Our hero awoke. After turning several times on the bed, the hidden rifle began to bother his back. A chill from the street and an opaque brightness through the partially open window announced daybreak. He looked for Sonia in the lodging. Even though he could take in the scene with just one glance, it took him awhile to realize he was alone. He stuck his feet out from under the blanket and stretched, irritated he'd slept with his boots on in addition to everything else. He situated his penis, shrunken by the cold and vodka, back in his pants and went over to close the window.

The mystic in the next-door room had finished his purgatory or dedicated himself to some other type of meditation. All was silent. It was a good moment to write. He searched the table for the bundle of papers of his novel. He insisted on going through everything again, because he didn't want to accept that the two coins were proof of a purchase. Vasili suspected there couldn't be another version of this story of a resentful woman, a novel, and two coins, except the one he didn't want to accept.

He threw the books on the bed, hoping Sonia had hidden the novel in one last prank. He searched through everything until he even lost sight of the two coins. From the window he looked for her, maybe she was walking around, hopping on the sidewalk in front like a finch.

St. Petersburg was awakening, white and ill mannered, just like every morning. Some offices were open, others weren't. Heads of women and old men came and went without exchanging greetings or insults. And at the top of the snow-covered roofs, the missing plank enabled Vasili to see the waiter's torso.

"What else would the man do, or even an extraordinary person do? Why else, did he just get angry and do it?" ponders the Reader at the next table, but quells his wandering thoughts so he can hear the end of the story.

Vasili removed the books he'd thrown on the bed, lifted the mattress, and took out the rifle. He didn't check the lone bullet, nor did he remember the afternoons hunting with his father. He hid behind the partially opened window, the exact width to stick the barrel out, and fired.

As he was putting the rifle away again, he found it comforting that the mystic hadn't started his prayers. He considered the lack of synchrony, nothing literary, a very good ending.

# B

That unknown vertex at the end of the bullet's journey, reasons the Reader, is no character other than Vasili himself.

The two men order another round, agreeing in a low voice that one of them will pay for the first vodkas and the other the second round. The Reader, who still hasn't finished his drink, listens to one man correct the other's story.

"Perfection," the man says, "has nothing to do with the story, except that chance perfection of the same shot. Sonia, the prostitute, lived in a rather high apartment, more solitary than a finch since her father's death. She'd been seeing Vasili for a while. And even though he'd promised to remove her from such a bad life, he took all the money she earned, because he was in debt with several editors who controlled him stingily with the promise of novels, whose submissions he always postponed. Sonia often saw him begin to write enthusiastically, only later to find him burning everything. He wasn't a writer, nor anything even close. Sonia became pregnant by Vasili. When she told him, he hit her brutally and stopped visiting. He started looking for work with some Tartars, who repaired roofs in St. Petersburg. The morning the Tartars were fixing the restaurant roof across the street, he didn't know if Sonia was still pregnant or had lost the baby in the beating. From her window she recognized the writer, took out a rifle she'd inherited from her father, and fired. However, she missed her target. Instead the bullet entered a gap between the boards that'd been moved for the repairs and killed a waiter."

Whether he prefers this version or the previous one, the Reader hasn't yet decided when he stands up, ready to return home, possibly to the building across the street. He leaves some coins on the table and swallows the last of his vodka, warming his throat as he leaves the tavern that looks hazy in the city's brightness.

Fine layers of snow cover everything, clinging to bushes and fences, distorting and disconnecting them more and more from their original form.

In her boring St. Petersburg routine of coming and going from one room to another, her only motivation was to locate every last hiding place of objects left by a previous tenant. In that way she was like a magpie, even though with a glance in the mirror she'd recognize herself as an agreeable, yet sad finch. Moving suddenly from a neighborhood wasn't something she'd set as a goal. The mornings of men already demanded enough without something else that made her walk through the streets from the port looking for companionship. But in St. Petersburg one employer after another was suddenly obliged to be away to visit her relatives in a gray province, causing her to have to move to another place, jumping from here to there deciphering some announcement on a door that offered a room for a guest. And there Sonia found dirty newspapers she could read and gloves with holes she caressed and sniffed. Sometimes she slid her hands into them and touched her breasts, bony hips, thighs, lying on the new lodging's floor.

When the door closed behind her, the room seemed excessively clean and she doubted she'd find a single new, old thing. Nevertheless, she got on her knees to look under the bed, where she discovered a suitcase near the headboard, against the wall.

It wasn't a heavy suitcase. Despite her best efforts, Sonia couldn't open it. She'd need some tools to break the locks' clasps. Sitting on the suitcase, she reckoned she could use it as a piece of furniture. First, she moved it over to the window to see if it'd be useful, but a chair was already there. Then, she placed it beside the table, even though she knew she wouldn't receive any guests. From there she discovered the view of the city her new room offered. Nothing special. St. Petersburg from the window looked as clean as the room itself.

You'll keep a suitcase too, thought Sonia to herself.

She dragged her new acquisition over to the armoire to help her climb up and look around. Perhaps she'd find a few cobwebs with some interesting deviation that'd make up for her disappointment about the secretive suitcase. When she placed her feet on the suitcase, the clasps and the lid sprang open unexpectedly and a package of papers fell out, spreading in a line across the floor.

*. . . 1865*

*My most excellent K:*

*May I possibly count on the publication of my little novel in* Russki Viéstnik? *These last two weeks I have been writing and am at the point of completion. It will be five or six pages. Two weeks of work lie before me, possibly more. However, by all means, I can faithfully assure you the novel shall be ready within a month. You shall have it, without fail, in your hands within that time.*

*As far as I can judge (in my humble opinion), this novel does not seem out of place in your magazine's style, but rather to the contrary. It is a psychological study of a crime. Time period: present day, this current year.*

Sonia traveled with few things. Her life was so agitated because of her frequent room changes that she never collected, much less found a place for the few items she did have. Only one thing came with her, despite the inconvenience when the time came to throw everything into a suitcase and bear its weight: a copper samovar she found once in a tavern's patio. It was broken, but Sonia drug it along. After some cleaning and repairing, the samovar shone and in it she prepared a strong tea as dark as ink.

Each time she arrived in a new room, after having inspected every nook and cranny for remnants, she found the best spot for the samovar and served her first cup of tea in the room. This time she positioned it on the table by the window. Moving it directly in front of her chair, she began the ritual of the inaugural sip. When the water had boiled, she opened the small faucet, covering the cup's bottom with dark tea. She warmed her hands, inhaled the steam that smelled like a graveyard, settled her feet on the chair, and took the first few letters from the package.

*February 18, 1866*

*. . . To begin with, I work as if I were a forced laborer. I am writing a novel for* Ruskii Viéstnik. *At the end of November, I had written and completed a great deal; however, I burned it all. Only now am I able to confess this. I did not care for it. A new configuration had occurred to me, a new plan, and consequently I began again from the beginning. I work day and night, and yet my efforts produce very little.*

*According to my calculations, each month I must send six pages to* Ruskii Viéstnik. *It is terrible, and I am only able to do this if I have the necessary calmness of spirit. A novel is a poetic work that requires one's dedication of complete tranquility of spirit and inspiration. And yet, the creditors pursue me relentlessly. Until today I was unable to reach an accord with them, and I do not know if I will succeed, even though many are reasonable and accept my offer to pay them in five years. But with the rest, I have yet to make arrangements.*

*On this occasion I will tell you about my current literary concerns and in this way you will see how things are. Finding myself hastened by the circumstances, I offered employment to K., at a price that is miserly for me, of one hundred twenty-five rubles per page.*

"Nothing near miserly for me," added Sonia.

*. . . Farther along I discovered that those people accepted*

*with pleasure, because they did not have writers for that year. Turgenev does not write, and they have had a falling out with Leo Tolstoy. Alongside them I appeared to be a conciliatory bastard (all of this I know on good authority), but they began to offer excuses and provoke me. Essentially, they are miserable people. The novel seemed wonderful and they were frightened of the idea of having to pay for twenty-five or thirty pages at one hundred twenty-five rubles per page.*

*To summarize: all their politics (on this we already agreed) are reduced to no more than ensuring that I reduce the price, while my efforts are to raise it. And now we are ensnared in a sort of rivalry . . .*

"In my opinion," said Sonia aloud, "they're sons of bitches."

After a long drink of tea, she continued reading.

*June 1866*

*My dear and respected Friend,*

*K. is summering in Petrovskii Park. L. (the director of Ruskii Viéstnik) is also on holiday. In the magazine's editorial office, there is no one aside from a bored clerk, who knows nothing. However, I was able to find L. in the first few days. He had already instructed that I write three chapters of my novel. I promised him I would write the fourth chapter at full gallop. The four chapters would complete exactly half of the end of the second part. However, before I could explain, L. spoke first, saying, "I have been waiting for you in order to inform you that now, in June and July, we are able to, and in actuality should, publish the novel in small quantities, even possibly suspending one of the later chapters, due to the times in which we find ourselves. We wish to do it in a way such that the second half of the novel appears in the autumn and its conclusion in the December issue, as the novel's influence shall motivate subscribers for the following year." And so, it was arranged that the publication of the novel shall be suspended for yet another month, and thus the four chapters (four pages) shall not be published until July and are, nonetheless, already written.*

*But later it became clear that L. had proceeded with a second scandalous intention. He did not want to publish one of the four chapters he had in his power, and K. confirms his decision. I have had an understanding with each of them, but they continue digging in their heels. Regarding the chapter in question, I am unable to say anything. I wrote it with sincere inspiration, but it is possible it came out wrong. Their criticisms do not concern the literary value, but rather the writing's morality. In that sense, it is I who is correct. The chapter contains nothing immoral, rather the complete opposite. However, they are of a differing opinion and even see in it the beginnings of nihilism. L. has expressed to me most emphatically that I must rewrite the chapter.*

Sonia put down the letter and picked up another one, saying to herself: "Don't redo anything . . . or redo, my dear. Completely. But they should pay you for both."

*January 12, 1868*

*. . . In summary, my life has proceeded in this manner. I have worked and been tormented. Do you know what it means to create? No, thank heavens that you do not know! From each project and similarly every line, I do not believe you have ever written or experienced that hellish nightmare. Upon accepting so much money in advance from* Ruskii Viéstnik *(a true horror of four thousand five hundred rubles), I came to believe that at the start of the year my muse would not leave me in a lurch. On the contrary, I trusted that poetic ideas would dazzle me and continue thus through to the year's end. As such I would be able to escape my many hardships. I held hopes of such a future. Alas, the thing never blossomed. Nothing. I spent summer and autumn fostering all sorts of ideas (some quite interesting), but*

*a certain experience made me feel dishonest or troubled to have so many ideas with such limited effort. Until finally I chose one idea and began to work. I had written a good deal when I sent the whole thing to the devil and tore the manuscript. I assure you the novel could not possibly have been accepted. But I suffered, and rightly so because the novel was merely average and not positively good quality. I wanted something else. What should I have done then? It is already December 4! But the circumstances of my life have conspired in the ensuing manner:*

*I do not know if I told you (I simply do not remember anything) that having exhausted all my resources, I wrote to K., pleading with him to send me one hundred rubles every month. I believe I did relate this to you already. He responded positively and has sent me money punctually. But in my letter to K. (the one in which I provided explanations), I promised him in a positive manner, under my word of honor, to send him the novel. And declared that by December he would have in his hands a considerable portion of the narrative. I was able to write that since work was going well and at that time I had written a considerable amount. Later I wrote to him again to say I had many expenses and to ask if he could possibly send me, instead of the agreed-upon amount (one hundred rubles), that if for just one time (for the month of December) he could send me two hundred rubles instead of one hundred. In December I received his response along with the money, and it arrived precisely when I had destroyed the manuscript.*

"Just imagine," said Sonia and served herself another cup of tea.

*January 13, 1868*
*Approximately three weeks ago I thought of another novel and began writing both day and night. The idea of the novel is an old one and it always enticed me; however, it is so difficult I never dared to develop the idea further. Only now did I choose*

*it, due to my desperate situation. In twenty-three days, I wrote the first part and have already sent it. It did not produce the desired effect. Naturally, it is a simple preface, which fortunately, in no way implicates the remainder of the novel. It explains nothing, not even suggesting a single dilemma. My only desire is to awaken the reader's interest, so that he continues to read the second part . . .*

When she finished reading the last page, Sonia remained still a little while longer, as if she were thinking or making herself believe what she thought. Her legs had been crossed and were stiff due to the cold, not having moved for some time. Among the pages of the draft letters were a few thick, unused pages, as well as a dirty fountain pen. Sonia took one of the pages and with the remaining tea from the old samovar wrote so many lines she filled the page without stopping. Returning the letters to the suitcase, in the same order in which she'd found them, she let her own page that she'd just written fall on top of the others before closing the lid.

The clasps closed tightly. Sonia pulled the suitcase back under the head of the bed, where it'd stay a long time until another curious person searched through the filth and obscurity of the great city's anonymous lodgings. Later, she took from her bodice a wrinkled piece of paper that held two pills, a legacy given to her by a prostitute who'd gotten married. They'd been a gift from an old lover, who was a pharmacist. Sonia had never found a need for them. The emptiness of her life had never reached a point for her to use them heroically, nor to throw them away. One of the pills was falling apart, so a few days before she'd decided to swallow them once and for all. The unexpected departure of her previous employer had returned her to the street and she postponed her decision.

She opened the window and breathed the dull St. Petersburg air. The sun was rising. She tossed the pills in her mouth and swallowed quickly, avoiding the taste that she'd notice if they brushed against her tongue. She waited a bit, watching the street and the heads of the old people and women. All the roofs covered in snow. In the tavern across the street, some men fixed a section of the roof.

She reached for the samovar and raised it up to the window. She made certain the path to the street was empty, not wanting to cause anyone harm. She only wanted to call attention so her body wouldn't pass a few days forgotten in the empty room and they'd only find her due to the bad odor. With all the strength she had left, Sonia threw the samovar, which hit with a loud noise in the mud and snow. Through the hole in the roof left by the repairmen, she saw the waiter slowly look up at her.

The pain shook her as if someone had shot her in the abdomen. She lay down on the bed. She didn't close her eyes, but instead distracted herself looking at the window. The emptiness of infinity helped her to maintain the memory of the man's glance. Waiting, she hummed an old song.

*Dear Author of these letters,*

*I discovered some of your adventures through a particular obsession of mine to search through everything. I have a few things to tell you if you have time to decipher my careless handwriting.*

*Consider that a novel, or whatever it may be, is nothing more than a half-closed window through which one sees a part of St. Petersburg, but it will never be the same St. Petersburg with its miseries and its slow smiles. Once I climbed a narrow ladder with a drunk man in the early morning and we balanced on the steps as if we were flying over the Neva River on a summer morning. I've never found this in a single novel, not in a single story. It happened and was lost forever. You're even able to tear a piece of this letter and use that passage as a scene in one of your stories, but they'll not be my hands covering my mouth to keep from waking the other tenants, nor Vasili's, which is the man's name, with his heavy boots climbing the stairs and squeezing my thighs above my skirt hem.*

*You'll probably resist listening to what I tell you. How would you not resist, since giving credit to my lines would abolish all your worries. But life isn't in literature, and you wasted all your time writing to make money, as if you were sowing potatoes. Writing night and day and later burning all your pages, imagining yet another way to improve the story, and later refusing to accept certain earnings that, according to you, were not deserved. What does that bring you, Mr. Author of those draft letters? Remember, the only things in this world that don't have a price are those that, in the end, no one wants to buy. Virtue isn't a useful thing, because it doesn't provide enough to live on, nor is it more than an obscene formula to distort reality. Something I do know, but can do nothing to change, is that the writer will always have the last word.*

*Life is more present in your letters than in your novels you sent to* Ruskii Viéstnik. *Although I haven't read a single one, it's enough to have lived a little to know about the anti-literary fortune that is all of life. Nevertheless, your letters postponed my death one night!*

*Now everything will end and I take this, my last step, as resentment against the man. I lived his manuscript pages and I became emotional about the fragments of his life as if they were one of his novels, possibly his best. Accept this as the postponement of a moment of clarity from someone at the edge of an abyss. Write, write a lot if life is not easy for you, and to others leave the weariness and suicide.*

*Sonia, a whore.*

# Epilogue

Snow is falling today, almost wet snow, yellow, dirty. It was snowing yesterday, too, and the other day. I think it is because of the wet snow that I remembered the incident which gives me no rest now.

Fyodor Dostoyevsky

\*

Perhaps it's normal in a city that extends between two continents to find all types of intersections. On a street corner in Istanbul, a group of friends was discussing the meaning of the word lampo. One of them said lampo was a unit of measure, possibly of weight or something else, but without doubt a unit no longer used. Maybe a unit of time. Another said it was a coin from a southern land. Another believed a lampo was a type of tailless, Asian rat that lives behind cheap restaurants, feeding off shriveled vegetables and fish tails. Its appearance isn't unpleasant; it resembles a very round hamster and is a light blue color, like a baby boy's cake. When they die, they float in the sewers like balls of yarn. At night in the gutters and by the piers, you can see their bodies drifting by like offerings or wet bread rolls or unfulfilled desires. Someone else agreed a lampo was an animal, but more like a jellyfish or anemone. If it touched your back or a thigh, it could cause a blister that'd leave a four-leaf-clover-shaped burn when it burst. Another man said that according to his grandparents and family, a lampo was a frying pan with a thoroughly flat bottom and a semispherical crack between the center and the edge, as if indicating seven o'clock when you held it by the handle. It was used to cook plain tortillas, which were different than the normal tortillas due to the slightly raised crease at the five o'clock marking when you flipped it onto a plate. And this small hill, a little more golden than the other parts, assured the guest the meal had been prepared in an authentic lampo. Someone else said a lampo was the subjective representation of an objective reality, manifesting itself as scents. More precisely, he continued, it was the recurrence of a certain smell, characterized by a reddish, plastic discharge that forms below the nostrils when the person experiences some daily event. It's so natural it only bothers the nose a bit. Of course, those lampos occur to some people more frequently than others. Another man said it'd happened to him, but he hadn't made the mistake of calling it lampo. He added it was merely an outbreak of rust on a dagger he'd kept for years as an artifact, which had once killed a very musically talented boy. The lampo, he added, is the bittersweet, diamond-like oxidation that forms like salt crystals on a sheet of metal, and if you tap it with your fingernail it makes a bell-like sound. Yet another man, sitting on the windowsill of his house, said the lampo was a sexually transmitted disease that could only be caught, God protect him, from practicing a com-plicated position in which the urethra reaches a negative angle, necessary for the semen to swim up or down, in the case that the man is infected or becomes a transmitter. To avoid exposing others to the uncertainty about the lampo, he wouldn't reveal the position, since the illness is fatal but asymptomatic, and the position results in a cruel addiction. Someone else said lampos (in the plural this time) were abstract particles located in elec-trons. Because of such accelerated vibrations, time and space were blurred. Nevertheless, they continued to be a hypothesis that provided evidence of other laws or the existence of certain particles that are indeed real and not lampo-like. Therefore, the lampos formed an intermediate dust that doesn't exist, but whose premise enables the drawing of an invisible man's features. One man simply repeated: Lampo, lampo . . . as if he recognized it, without knowing what it was. Another person said a lampo was a haircutting tool from the time of barber surgeons; a time which otherwise made perfect sense. The lampo was a device made out of a cylindrical piece, with a carving-decorated handle and a bristled tip. What was difficult now was to determine if it'd been used on hair or to operate on a molar. However, in the end, it's of no importance, since the lampo exhibits its rebellious, fu-turistic, and diligent form, which confirms there's nothing more unproductive than a predetermined function. And yet another person had heard talk of the Lampo exclusively as a Golem, or imaginary creature, that two prostitutes from Berlin created in the early days of the First World War to scare themselves before going to sleep. The Lampo arrived in the form of a dwarf that appeared just at bedtime to demand they recite the adventures of the trickster Till Eulenspiegel, while they jumped from one mattress to the other until he grew tired of hearing stories and left only to return the next night. One prostitute said to the other: "The Lampo is coming!" Then they covered their heads with tattered quilts, consequently exposing their feet. They hurried to cover them, peeped their heads out, laughed, and only then could they fall asleep. Someone else said lampo was the specific moment, which only political refugees can confirm, when the sun is setting and a weak light emanates from the horizon, obscuring and erasing the view of the barbed-wire fences. In that instant, the men and women, upon looking at that sun in full lampo, feel they are and are not free.

"Books exist that are volumetric and three-dimensional, while others are hyper-volumetric and multidimensional," confessed a Greek stripper to me, as she prepared for a performance. "The former may or may not be hypnotic, but it'll always be possible to keep turning the pages with the certainty of gravitational force. It's possible to go down the stairs, invade their mansions, and move from one room to another through a vaulted-ceiling hallway. You could even gaze at them from outside, from their gardens, to confirm the battlements' jagged geometry with the absolute conviction that every brick is in its appropriate place and that the expression 'every brick' isn't madness. On the other hand, with hyper-volumetric books," she said, as she licked her lips, "one could stop reading, skip pages, forget about it, or begin on any line, because those books never hypnotize. And once inside, the expression 'every brick' is an error of agreement, because there could be stairs, where previously there was a room with an ocean view, and now there's a hungry fish and the vaulted-ceiling hallway leads back into itself like a doughnut. The castle with its battlements is more like a filing cabinet riddled with bullet holes. Something similar to automatic writing," she said, as she went on stage, "but on another level it could be affectionately called automatic fiction."

When I asked her about her job, she responded, "The center is immobile, but miniscule. It's irresistible, because it's an endeavor that involves a lot of production and is never-ending. And you know you'll have to continue struggling with it for many years to come. Just like the *Star Trek* saga, the second trilogy of *Star Wars*, or the entirety of *Harry Potter*. How do you resist when a champion Greco wrestler tries to assault you?"

In Alexandria, a boy who showed me to the hotel warned me, without me even asking:

"You won't find a single library here. A long time ago this was a city where books used to be raised like towers, only later to be burned in magnificent conquests. Afterward, entire libraries were presented to console a woman, but of those only memories remain. The people have learned to carry the volumes with them, catastrophe-proof."

Alone in the room, a sense of certainty ran through me. I visualized an empty highway in the distance and at the same time realized my journey was extremely irresponsible. Not only my journey, but also my determination to discover and stay in each Library. This search couldn't nor shouldn't be otherwise, nor did I want it to be different. In its own way, it showed a rejection of affection for, as well as an attack on tranquility of, those who once loved me and maybe still wait to hear from me. I was a young writer and wanted to travel: Jack Kerouac, I recalled.

That night in the hotel room, I wrote another book and left it with the porter to give to the boy. He was the Fourth Library.

# Book IV: The Book of the Beast
# Eternal Love
# for Jim Jarmusch

*Beast's power is so great, that I have no hopes of your overcoming him.*
Leprince de Beaumont

# 1

I'VE LOST MY SON. It's been years since I've known his where-abouts. He doesn't write or call. Eleven years after he left, a post-card arrived for me. Maybe I should say for us, since the family has increased and now includes two grandchildren, the children of my other two sons. Looking at them, I think: they don't even know their uncle. It was a blue postcard, partly cloudy. It showed a Gothic church being restored. Above the pinnacles hovered two yellow, rather fragile-looking cranes, which seemed ready to fall over at any moment. I don't know why, but it occurred to me that if such a catastrophe happened, my son would be in danger. Sometimes I assumed he operated one of the cranes, while at other times, as I was falling asleep, I imagined my diligent son in a cassock, inspecting the temple repairs and running back and forth like an old, emaciated sacristan who'd ascend to heaven when the cathedral collapsed like a sand castle. On the back of the postcard, he'd written: *All is well. Relax. Hugs.* My son, the writer. It's impossible to say my son, the writer, without a little bit of irony. Without a bit of guilt.

It all began (or became worse) with my trip to Rio de Janeiro. A trip for business and pleasure, it was a means to compensate myself in a way others never would. I'm a doctor. In Rio, during the summer of 1999, there was a surgeons' conference, whose last objective was to listen to guest speakers. It was a unique year and the end of the millennium was arriving like a risky operation that'd failed. The sessions, far from proposing technologies and intervention strategies, concentrated on the discussion of difficult cases and how the specialist successfully overcame the obstacles. Many attendees enjoyed the intermissions more than the talks, as they walked through the gardens, enjoyed a drink, and speculated about the new century. Rio, situated as if it'd fallen from the heavens and landed between the bay and Christ Redeemer with his open arms, presented itself as a city that'd accept everything and everyone. When I first saw it, I figured a city that built a Christ statue that tall must've seen the devil once.

I stayed at a colonial-style hotel in the historic district. I remember even the most trivial details: the sparkle of the chandeliers, the weathered wood, and the hospitable, yellow tone. The first night I decided to stay in my room to rest. It was Thursday. I watched a movie on television about a young man from New York, who hosts his cousin from Budapest for a few days. The girl is on her way to Cleveland, where they have an aunt. They eat and watch television. He introduces her to one of his friends. After a few days, the girl packs her bags. The cousin has grown fond of her. He gives her a dress and offers to walk her to the station, but she doesn't think it's necessary and leaves alone. She throws the dress in a trash can. A short time later, the young man and his friend swindle a few card players out of some money and travel to Cleveland in a borrowed car to visit the cousin. They find her. She works selling hotdogs. They walk around. They look at the snow. They don't talk much. As they're saying goodbye, one of them gets the idea to go to Florida. The three leave in the car and take many detours. Toward the end of the movie, the girl is walking alone by a stream, where a drug trafficker confuses her with someone else and gives her a package of money. I didn't completely understand the movie. I didn't know if I liked it or not. I took some time to find a comfortable position on the bed and then reviewed the story in my head (. . . *a young man in New York hosts a cousin from Budapest in his house for a few days*), searching for meaning until I fell asleep.

# 2

On Friday I ate lunch with a surgeon from Sydney and a Brazilian anesthetist. The man from Sydney showed us a picture of his mistress, a thirty-year-old blonde with a face incapable of pleasure. The Brazilian said she was a beautiful young woman and I agreed before giving him the photo back. Then the anesthetist passed around a photo.

"This is Duda," he said, "my son."

Sydney and I exchanged looks, wondering if the anesthetist was showing us his son or confessing he was gay. Although, in fact, he could've been both gay and presenting his son to us. His son wasn't unattractive, plus, the photo looked like it'd been taken after a lengthy sexual encounter. The situation had turned a bit awkward, so I decided to show pictures of my children. I was careful to first say:

"These are my three sons." I told them I was a widower, my sons lived with me, and the oldest two were doctors, like us.

"And this one, what does he do?" insisted the anesthetist.

"He's a writer," I told him. The man dropped the photo as if it'd burned his fingers.

"They seem like nice boys," said Sydney. I don't know if he perceived the tension.

"They are," I responded. The Brazilian anesthetist didn't say anything else.

That night I watched another movie in my room. An Italian woman is returning by plane to Rome with her husband's cadaver. Because of some problem, she has to spend the night in Memphis. Before looking for a hotel, she goes into a café. A man sits down in front of her and tells her that a year ago he was traveling at night in the outskirts of the city and kept seeing people who wanted a ride. Gradually he began to realize they were all the same person. He decided to stop and pick up the man, who was none other than Elvis Presley. According to the man, Elvis's ghost had given him a comb for the Italian woman. She accepts the comb and laughs at the story. The man tells her his passenger had told him she'd pay twenty dollars for the delivery. The woman hands him a bill so he'll leave. That night, while sharing the hotel room with a woman she didn't know, Elvis's ghost appears to her. The next day she takes a plane and flies to Rome with her dead husband. I didn't completely understand the movie and I didn't know if I liked it or not. I felt uncivilized and dated. I found the comfortable position I'd discovered for the new bed, then amused myself by searching for the story's meaning (. . . *an Italian woman flies to Rome with her husband's cadaver*), until I fell asleep.

# 3

Saturday morning I passed by a street vendor, who was singing "How Sad Venice Can Be" in Portuguese. I thought about my own loneliness, but thanked life for such a rational existence. I was grateful for my work, but in all honesty I was thankful for my status. The colonial district was easy to walk around, with its traditional streets and idyllic markets. I recall the place had a somewhat gaudy feeling about it, but at the same time it was so authentic I became emotional and my eyes welled up. That afternoon, after four narcissistic seminars, I escaped with Sydney to buy a few gifts. My colleague needed to find a purse for his mistress and I had three requests from my sons. The oldest had asked for a fountain pen. The middle son a wristwatch.

"You should visit the National Library," my youngest had recommended, "it's the largest in Latin America." After his multiple attempts to avoid the subject, I finally got him to ask for something. It wasn't difficult to guess he'd ask for a book. When he said so, his brothers teased him. He said it was a rather unknown book, which I probably wouldn't be able to find. He suggested if I had time to take a walk about the city, I could ask a bookseller on the street about it.

My son, the writer. Ever since he was a child, he'd read for hours, no matter the time of day. Sometimes I thought he was sick and that he continued to suffer from his mother's death. I insisted he go outside to play with other boys his age and come home at night like his brothers. You won't have memories of your childhood, I'd tell him. When time goes by and you look back, you won't have any memories except those words and being closed up in your room. At that time he still spoke a little. He told me what he read about. When he turned fifteen, he stopped talking. He announced he was a writer or he'd become one sooner or later. It seemed to us like a run-of-the-mill decision. And yet, he said it as if it were a curse, as if he'd been diagnosed with some kind of illness. He stopped talking to us; we didn't exist to him. And, if he happened to notice us, he looked like he was saying goodbye. He changed overnight. He stopped brushing his hair and always wore the same clothes. He never stopped reading. In his room he listened to sad songs. He wrote in a notebook with worn covers, which he always kept with him. Once one of his brothers managed to glance through it. Even though I scolded him for violating his brother's privacy, I couldn't resist the temptation to ask him what he'd found.

"Our brother is sick," he said. "Our brother is absolutely crazy. Our brother is a writer."

And I loved him more and more. His secrecy pained me and I believed I should protect him. I came to realize I loved him above all else, even more than my other sons, whose decision to follow in my medical footsteps and frequent conversations about their studies made me very proud.

"You have to take a chance on something," he said to his brothers one day, interrupting their discussion as he left the table. "You have to risk it all."

Finding the pen and watch was easy. Sydney, as if he were following directions on a map, carried a page from a magazine advertising the purse. In a boutique a saleswoman took the paper, smiled at him, and returned with the actual handbag. We accomplished our tasks rather quickly. Sydney offered to accompany me on my book search, hoping to find something to read on the trip home. We discovered a two-story bookstore. While Sydney went to the second floor, I approached a salesman and asked about the book. He said it'd be difficult to find in a bookstore and suggested I ask one of the booksellers on the street or in a store for old books.

"Here, as you can see, we only have the latest publications. And at present, I don't know what's going on with these, but to tell you the truth, I don't recommend a single one."

Sydney came downstairs to tell me he'd stay longer, because he'd met a girl he wanted to spend some time with until he got her back to his hotel room. He begged me to take his purchase with me, for fear his new conquest might take a liking to the gift. I took it and left in search of a street bookseller. A large, dirty dog was sprawled on the sidewalk. As it scratched behind its ear, its face resembled a thinker. I'd completed two purchases and was walking around with the purse for the woman incapable of pleasure. Tired, I decided to return to my room and continue my search the next day. In the morning we'd attend the closing ceremony, a toast, and a farewell, which wouldn't last long. As I walked by the dog, it stopped scratching to look intently at me.

I watched a cowboy movie on television. A young accountant travels to a faraway town in the West for work. When he arrives, he finds the town follows its own rules and at the factory they'd already hired someone else for his job. Curiously, the young accountant's name is William Blake. That night he meets a prostitute and sleeps with her. In the morning the woman's lover breaks into the room and, seeing her with another man, kills her with one shot. Blake shoots her lover and flees the town. The dead man turns out to be the factory owner's son and the old man hires three famous hitmen to capture the newcomer. Blake meets an Indian named Nobody in his escape through the desert. Nobody has had enough schooling to know who Blake is. The Indian keeps insisting the accountant is a poet and in his new life his poems are bullets. Thus, Blake shoots all who cross his path, but he also collects lead in his body. When the shots he's received make Blake very weak, Nobody says his farewells and sends him down the river in a canoe. On that last journey, William Blake will find his place in good time. Occasionally it seemed like a macabre story of a life that deforms into the supernatural. In other moments it reminded me of a worn-out superstition (. . . *a young accountant travels to a faraway town out West for work*). Why do they make these movies? I ask myself.

# 4

The closing toast was more boring than an appendicitis operation. The surgeons didn't listen to the other doctors, who, in turn, weren't interested in speaking in public to their colleagues. Nonetheless, the general mood was one of conformity. Sydney emerged from the multitude:

"We have to meet so I can pick up the purse."

I told him I planned to leave the conference room as soon as possible, because I still had to visit a couple bookstores.

"I'll pass by your hotel and leave it there." Sydney also wanted to escape. He was to have lunch with the girl he'd met the day before and then have another roll in the hay before flying to Australia.

Most of the surgeons' hotels were very close to each other. I told the receptionist at Sydney's hotel that he should give the purse to Sydney personally when he asked him for it. If he saw him arrive with someone else, he should only tell him someone had left something for him. My insistence seemed to cause him to look warily at the purse, as he picked it up by both handles and placed it within sight. At that very moment, Duda, the anesthetist's son, walked down the stairs.

"Good morning, Paul," he said to the receptionist. "If they call me, I'll be in the café for a bit reading." Duda lifted up the book in his hand. In doing so, he seemed to add to the greeting or emphasize he'd be reading. The book was the same one I was seeking for my son.

The café was connected to the hotel, to the side and behind a pair of wooden doors carved with vines and flowers. At this hour, it was empty, dimly lit, and smelled of herbs. The same vegetable motifs ran through the front window's opaque glass, beyond which one could glimpse dim shadows of people walking by. Very quietly, as if whispered in the ear, an American ballad played. "When a Man Loves a Woman." Again, the music made me sad and I felt completely abandoned. An apathetic employee tended the bar. Duda had positioned himself behind a table and was already reading. I ordered a coffee and approached him.

"Good afternoon," I said. He took his time before looking up from the book, as if waiting until the end of a paragraph, which reminded me of my younger son's indifference. The employee brought me my coffee and even though Duda still hadn't acknowledged my presence, I said:

"Excuse me," and sat down at his table. He closed the book and gave me a lethal look. The image of him in the photograph I'd seen came to mind.

"Sorry," I said. "I just wanted to ask you where I can get a book like yours."

"Why would someone like you want a book like this?"

"It's not for me. It's for my younger son. He asked me for the book as a gift."

"How old is your son?"

"Seventeen."

"Is he already a writer?"

"That's what he says," I answered, but at the same time I realized I hadn't told him anything else about my son. "Are only writers interested in this book?"

"Let's say only young writers," Duda responded and he adjusted a few locks of hair that'd fallen across his forehead. "Young writers and their parents," he joked before taking out a pen and writing an address on a napkin. "This store sells old books. It's not always open."

"I'll go tomorrow."

"You're not suggesting I sell you mine, are you?" he added, not looking at me. "I hope you're successful."

I didn't know the anesthetist's name, nor was I sure whether he was Duda's father or lover, but I decided to mention him to justify my abrupt approach.

"The anesthetist mentioned you to me," I said, standing up. His eyes changed, as he shrunk back like a cat and tossed the book on the table.

"Does he know I'm here?"

"No," I assured him vehemently. "I promise. I found you purely by accident." I told Duda I was a doctor and had come to Rio for a surgeons' conference. I'd met the man there (I didn't want to repeat "the anesthetist" again), who'd shown me his photo after I'd shown him one of my children. I inverted the order of the photos to avoid involving the component of sexual ambiguity that surrounded the situation, since with each passing moment I was less certain of the relationship between them. I sat back down, believing it was my responsibility to calm him down. Of course I was wrong. I told Duda about my other two sons, who are doctors. He asked me about my wife.

"She died many years ago."

"What do surgeons' wives die of?"

I responded that they die of boredom and he apologized for

asking. I then apologized for bothering him. I assured him the chances of me encountering the man again were minimal since the conference had ended a few hours before and I'd leave the next day.

"Have you seen him today?" Duda asked. I didn't remember saying goodbye to him. It seemed the anesthetist hadn't been among all the handshakes and farewells, so I told him I hadn't.

"In that case, go to the address I gave you. It doesn't matter to me if you tell him you saw me. I won't stay here a minute longer."

I took out some coins to pay for the coffee and then decided to take my cup back to the bar. I wanted to leave the table just as Duda had it, as if I'd never been there. He was peering out the window through the designs on the glass. He murmured something, which might not have been what I actually heard, since young people use a different language and sometimes Portuguese sounds like a moan. "It's a beast," I think he said.

I had no idea how close or far the address was that he'd given me. I stopped a taxi. Once inside I handed the napkin to the driver, and I swear he did everything possible for the wind to snatch it from his hand, when he returned it to me right beside the window. The silky paper flew away before I could grab it.

"Are we going to a parking garage?" he asked me.

"It's a bookstore," I said while looking at the buildings we passed, and deliberately bid farewell to the city.

"Are you sure, friend?"

"It's a place where they sell used books," I responded.

"Very old ones," he laughed. "Please don't be mad about the lost napkin." Turning to look at me and not paying attention to the road, he added, "An address written in a hurry belongs to a place you'll only visit once."

The building, just like the block of parking garages it actually was, had long, spiral balconies. Once in a while, I could see a car driving by, looking for a place to enter or leave. I walked across the deserted first level, where I found a sleeping dog, some boxes, and a damaged tire. I thought the taxi driver had ripped me off and taken me somewhere else. I walked between the columns until I found a bookcase leaning against a wall at the back. Beside it a stairway led down to the basement. The metal gate was open and I figured that meant I could go down. I paused to look at the books beside the entrance. Several discolored magazines, an anthology of French science fiction, and a few books in English. As soon as I touched one of the volumes, I heard footsteps behind me. An old man who looked like a mechanic walked toward me, followed by the dog that'd shaken off his lethargy.

"All those are the same price," he called to me. I asked him about the book I was looking for and told him someone had assured me I'd find it here.

"Go on down then," he responded. "All who come here look for what they want by themselves and later we negotiate the price." I went down the stairs. When I glanced up, I noticed the dog had moved closer to watch my descent.

What I saw below calmed me down. It was an open space that once had belonged to the same garage and was now divided by bookshelves and long tables, as if various libraries had been unloaded there. The place was well lit, with windows along the walls at sidewalk height, where you could see people walking by. Three young people examined books on a table. A girl and two boys. None of them paid me any attention and I didn't want to ask them anything. They might try to disorient me, if by chance they were after the same book.

On the most organized bookshelves, I came across surgical books in French and German that I recognized from citations. Several times I reprimanded myself as I lost minutes caressing their pages. I had the impression that, little by little, the young people began to follow my same route, as if we were in fact after the same book. Since I wanted to find what I was looking for as quickly as possible and the bookstore offered no strategy other than coincidence, I consequently focused on searching the most inaccessible places. Everywhere I looked I found a blue tome titled *The Dancing Goshawk*. The young people seemed to be competing openly with me. Other people started appearing out of nowhere. The sun had set. It was hot. The dust in the air burned my throat and the humidity caused fragments of old book covers to fall apart in my hands. Everything was quiet. I had no other choice but to trust I'd found a rather busy section. I sweated. If I blinked, things seemed to change color. It was as if I were looking through a piece of red glass. I blinked and then everything turned magenta. After squeezing my eyelids tightly, my vision returned to normal. An old lady walked by with a grocery cart full of books; she smiled at me as she walked away. I saw a doctor from the conference and to avoid greeting him I turned down another aisle. I entered a door that led to a corridor, from which I could see many more books piled up on the floor. I saw an anatomy book from my time at the university and became alarmed, because all of a sudden I remembered that the colleague I'd fled from hadn't been at the conference. I knew him when I was at school. I thought he'd died.

I have to escape from here, I thought. I'll leave the city early tomorrow. My suitcase is packed. I've bought a pen and a watch for my sons, the doctors. I must flee from this hell.

I didn't want to return the way I'd come. This corridor will take me somewhere, I told myself, repeating it later as if I were begging it to be true. The bookshelves had fallen and books were stacked clumsily, some atop others, open, twisted, in pieces. You couldn't see the floor, because it was covered by more books than I could move with my feet or climb over. There's no image more disturbing than a mountain of books and people rummaging through it. That's exactly what I saw when I looked behind me, before the door closed violently. In front of me, the aisle became darker and I moved forward on my hands and knees. When I paused, I became delirious. I saw Sydney fornicating with the woman from the second floor of the bookstore, the one I never met, but I knew it was she. I saw the Australian mistress sleeping inside her new purse. I saw Duda cutting down a tree. I saw for a second time the three movies I'd seen night after night in my head before I fell asleep. I saw my wife without a single feature of her decomposed body that could remind me of her; nevertheless, it was she. She yelled to me:

"Don't go outside the circle. Don't even put one foot outside of it."

Already by then, I think I was being pulled. I was short of breath and completely naked. I moved wet books that fell apart like mud. It felt like I was moving forward on the tiled roof of a convent. Disintegrating tiles or recently made tiles. Marks embedded themselves into my hands and looked like spots from a mortal illness that climbed up my arms and around my neck, then spread to my face. Sometimes I experienced moments of lucidity in which I believed I was dreaming, at other times I totally lost the capacity to think rationally and saw my hands disappearing into the books. Clinging to the temporary stability of the rational moments, I used that brief impulse to press onward. It felt as if the glue of the pages was running through my fingers. This is what my son, the writer, aspires to, I realized. He wants to convert himself into this. He wants to submit himself to this.

I began to touch bottom. Little by little the books started to vanish and I reached the edge of the concrete floor. I heard cars moving at full speed somewhere above my head, which made me think that, despite everything, I was still in the parking garage. A large dirty window allowed me to see people passing by on the sidewalk above. With the limited light, I was able to see a yellow circle drawn on the floor like a border of separation. It's the circle my wife told me about, I thought, and without hesitation moved to the center. Once I was there, the pedestrians stopped moving by the windows. I didn't hear any more cars on the floor above. Night fell.

At first there was a somewhat bland, irritating smell, like fermented lemons. A lightbulb flickered twice before it turned completely on. Then the whole place filled with the unbearable smell of burned garbage. I turned around, trying to orient myself, and what I saw in the corner paralyzed me. I checked to see if my feet were still inside the circle. That thing came closer to me. It moved as if each step required a great deal of concentration or effort. The smell came from him. It looked like it might fall as it swayed. It occurred to me that if it fell down all would be lost. Although at that moment I didn't know exactly what I was referring to with such a concept of totality, nor what it could aspire to in the future, nor to what type of peace. The world will be terrible, I thought. My naked body trembled and at the same time I couldn't feel a single muscle. It burned my eyes to look at it, and yet, I couldn't look away. In its ghastly appearance, in addition to the grotesque anatomical deviations, it also exhibited a morbid purpose. It ended up hanging around the edge of the circle. With an extremity, it handed me the book I'd been looking for. I still remember its voice:

"Here's the book, but you may not take it with you. Tell your son his copy exists. He must come for it himself."

*

In Karachi I paused in front of a snake charmer. He was taking a break and the cobra rested curled up inside the basket. He admitted to me that tourists weren't satisfied anymore to just see the cobra dance.

"Now they want to bring the snake home with them," he said. "If you want to know the truth, the cobra doesn't actually dance. It follows the movements of the flute with its head. That's the true charm and it appears to dance because its damn body always ripples."

He handed me the flute in case I wanted to try it and left me to care for his basket. I looked around to ensure no one would see me making a snake dance in Pakistan. I raised the basket's lid, lifted the flute without playing it, and the cobra began to rise up. Instead of having it move side to side, I had it extend upward; the cobra remained straight. Then, it looked away from the flute and stared me directly in the eyes. Flaring its hood like a weightlifter flexes his muscles, it said:

"Has it never surprised you how within a group of friends or a family the memory of a trivial event from years ago lingers and gets brought up every time the group is together? The story can center on a phrase, a nickname, or some word that is incomprehensible to someone outside the group. Have you ever taken a step back and felt bewildered by the absurd repetition that has no humor or impact? These measly efforts are an attempt to resist the passage of time, death's human vertigo."

I lowered the flute and the cobra collapsed upon itself.

At some point during the trip, I became troubled by the appearance of certain spies. Strange agents who approached me to engage in conversation and disorient me.

"Honestly, I was never inspired by postmodernity," said a man sitting by me on the train. "Other similar phenomena occur on a minor scale and are unnoticed. And that ghost is old. When I was a boy, I heard a story that summarizes in many ways the virtues of that age of humanity: In a town in the middle of nowhere that dominates Romania, a castle rose up at the edge of the cliff. In the castle, which appeared to be abandoned, there lived a count who often went down to the town to seize a virgin girl. The girls he abducted were converted into vampires. The girls' boyfriends, along with the parents of both the girls and the boyfriends, marched against the count, attempting to rescue the girls. But they too ended up converted into demonic beings in the count's service. Over the years, there were no more village girls, nor their suitors, parents, and parents-in-law. The town was reduced to a small group of unmarried, old women, who were also dying off. The count was so bored in the castle that he ordered the multitude of people housed in his collection of coffins to return to the village and pretend they'd been kidnapped and bitten for the first time."

The man seated in front of us lifted his head from the little César Aira book he was reading and commented:

"We have no way to prove it, but one can deduce that a certain series of events was made up by another. If you have good judgment, it's best not to try to unravel it all. It'd become even more complicated. Until the moment when we discover a thread, a short thread that ends, then we have to be convinced of what we want. If we pull on it, the yarn ball will unravel into a vacuum."

I stumbled upon a game room in Bombay behind a movie theater on a narrow, poorly lit street, like the ones you read about in cheap novels. There were few clients, who didn't seem to play anything. From a hidden place, some disco-like music announced the city was no longer called Bombay, but rather Mumbai and that we were all happy in Mumbai. Balancing on a large cushion, a woman guarded a second entrance protected by a colorful, beaded curtain.

"I recommend you enter the betting room," she said, winking with her third eye, and opened the curtain.

In the small hall, I found a table with three players. I would've preferred to ignore the invitation to fill the fourth chair, but they included me enthusiastically in the second hand. An unknown player's arrival commences a game with new rules.

One player leaned over to fix the wobbly table with a crumpled-up piece of paper, shaped in a sphere. The man to his left took advantage of the situation to look at the other's cards and then waited for the first man to sit back up before playing his hand:

"Samuel Hope lived until he was sixteen years old in a small town near Australia's Blue Mountains," he said as he carefully fanned his cards, as if each should be only partially visible. "During a business trip to Melbourne after his father's death, he spent a night with a woman twice his age. After a few days, he moved in with her and started working at a newspaper. Some months later he started a literary supplement that increased the newspaper's sales figures, leading it to be one of the most read papers by the literary elite. The following year he launched his own magazine and after four successful issues, he published a book of poems: *Happy Visits*. The collection garnered acclaim far and wide, so much so that he could count on one foot the number of people who didn't know from memory the verses that'd given the book its title. In April, his autobiographical novel appeared: *18 Years and 3 Hours*. Readers hadn't even had time to digest the hefty book, when he entered the second floor of the same publisher with a manila envelope containing a book of short stories: *Almost Summer*. The book exceeded the editors' expectations and they considered it a masterpiece. At that time the woman twice his age abandoned him for a man twice her age and flew to Los Angeles on a honeymoon from which she never returned. Unexpectedly, Hope cancelled the contract with the editors. It was never determined why, whether from the emotional abyss left by his cosmopolitan passion or the perfection of the volume he'd just finished. He dedicated most of his money to preventing the book's publication. With the remainder he bought a small beach house, where he lived the rest of his rather long life and ran a small fishing store. The sunsets, which were quite intense on the blue coast, never succeeded in diminishing his melancholy. The poet and autobiographer died one morning on the beach, where he lay for several hours until people realized he wasn't sunbathing."

The man closed his fan of cards and looked at the other players with intrigue, boasting of his hand. The one who'd placed the wedge under the table leg simply said:

"I pass."

And the man to his right lowered his head and said: "I pass."

I looked at my cards again and was obliged to play.

"On the outskirts of Tokyo," I said, "the author Higuchi Ichigo grew up. He made a living as a paid assassin, of great accuracy. He kept six drawers of a wooden chest full of his papers, drawings, and writings, which he added to each morning when he awoke and took pleasure in observing the abandoned blocks of buildings. Once the chest was filled and there wasn't room for a single page more, he threw the chest in the trash. The piece of furniture caught the attention of a woman who was returning from a long trip with her family. She insisted her husband stop and then, with difficulty, he got it into their little truck. Their son cried the rest of the way home. Noticing the piece of furniture, Nagi Aya had followed a strong intuition. After placing it in her study, she found it to be absolutely falling apart and outdated. Aya worked as an editor for the publishing house Shueisha and didn't waste time in composing her first novel based on one of the drawer's contents and a few pages from another. Ichigo, who didn't read much, never found out the acclaimed book *Goodbye and Thank You* was a work of his own writing. It was so successful that within a few months Aya sold the rights to Madhouse, Inc., which didn't take long to produce a movie and start arrangements on a video game for Wii.

"On assignment, Ichigo was sneaking up behind his victim, a businessman who was resting in his house watching an anime, when he recognized a dialogue he'd written. He held the sword in midair, just at the point of touching the man's skin, and remained there a moment contemplating the scene. The businessman laughed at the TV anime. His head rolled on the floor, creating a frame of blood. It was easy to find Nagi Aya early one morning editing another drawer of papers from the chest, by the geometric light from a paper lamp. When her son started crying in his room, she left the drawings to attend to him. It took her a long time to realize her crying son was pulling at the hair of his father's mutilated head. Her husband's body rested beside the bed, as if he were dreaming about being lost in a French garden. Ichigo jumped down from the ceiling and raised the point of his sword to the editor's chin.

"'The trash of others should be regarded with the same solemnity as the ashes of ones deceased,' he said. She would've responded that she'd acted based on an uncertain destiny, that she'd never denied publicly the existence of an unknown author, that the new mansion and all the savings belonged completely to him, that they could get married and live together with her small son, that she could continue to edit his novels, and that if he wished, if he couldn't break away from this obsession in order to continue writing his stories, that he could continue as a hit man. Nonetheless, she didn't say anything, because what she heard in a flurry about trash and ashes struck her like an incomprehensible verdict. It sounded something like her husband was trash and she should spread his ashes. On the other hand, the assassin, who forced her to support her body at the point of a sword, didn't remind her for a second of the author of those memorable papers she'd edited, but rather of an authentic Shinigami. Before she died, she glimpsed her husband lost in the French garden and saw herself converted into a ghost that terrified her, their paths crossing between dense, green leaves. Then, Ichigo set fire to the wooden chest. The little boy was never found. For a long time, the rumor existed that a baby walked around laughing in front of those who'd died decapitated."

The woman with the third eye had pushed her large cushion inside the room and, from the surprised reactions, it appears none of us had noticed her. Stroking the teardrops of one of the curtain strings, she joined the betting:

"Elijah was nine years old when he stowed away on a pirate ship. His parents had died in an accident in Morocco and the boy crossed the Atlantic on a ship headed for Bristol, where he'd be met by his uncle, who wasn't aware of all the disasters. However, the ship was intercepted en route by an infamous black flagship. On the pirate ship, Elijah was treated like a museum piece because of his young age and there were assumptions about the potential ransom they could collect once they found his relatives. A prostitute, who took on the task of making the arrangements, surprised the uncle in his office evaluating some topographical maps before going to bed. He didn't seem to understand much about the drawings.

"'Buying land isn't always a good idea,' said Miss Sunset.

"The uncle rambled senselessly about the woman's appearance, her defamation of his home, the late hour, and other threats to which she responded with a mocking laugh, like a colorful parrot.

"'This house is more accessible than a provincial brothel. If a woman waits until a certain hour to surreptitiously enter your most sacred room, don't you think she has something important to say?'

"She then turned toward the window spanning the entire back wall and concentrated on the night's scenery, as if she were trying to identify the exact spot on River Avon where the pirate ship was hiding.

"'All the passengers aboard the . . . oh, what was that magnificent boat called? Well, anyway, the boat from Morocco your nephew was traveling on. They're all dead. Some friends of mine, who had a hand in the submersion, which they refer to as a marvel of the complicated technique known as premeditated sinking, were kind enough to rescue the boy.'

"'One who's born to hang will never drown,' muttered the uncle, returning to his previous questions and accusations.

"Miss Sunset shut him up with a haunting parrot-like screech. 'The boy's worth his weight in gold. He's going to be a writer. You can see it in the way he walks around the ship's bow, looking at the sea's vastness with distrust. He's going to be a good one too. He saw a man go by him dragging a barrel and it didn't occur to him to help the man, instead he watched him as if he were studying him.'

"'For God's sake,' said the uncle, 'you're the first pirate I've seen who talks so positively about a mental illness. And I say that considering you're the first pirate I've met in my whole life.'

"'I'm not a pirate,' said Miss Sunset. 'I'm a prostitute who visits vessels of certain friends, who compensate me with valuable coins. They pick me up from a small boat with my name tattooed on the stern and that's how I board the ships, treated like no woman you'll ever meet. Your boy is a writer. He doesn't know it yet, of course, for now he's content defying the queasiness caused by the ocean's rolling. When he saw me, he held my gaze for fifteen seconds, something even you haven't been able to do.'

"'The weight of your friends' money confuses you,' said the uncle. 'My nephew will be a burden, but send him here any night you wish.'

"Miss Sunset strolled around the room to study the vulnerable points and approach the maps with imprudence. She didn't understand them either. Then she announced the price he'd have to pay for Elijah. Not a coin more or less.

"'I don't plan to throw away a single coin for a nephew who's a writer.'

"'Those who sent me won't welcome this response. Just think about it. They didn't let him drown in the premeditated sinking, they fed him this whole time, he's learned to tie knots . . .'

"'Tell your friends I'm in the business of land and I'm not interested in anything that comes floating in from the sea. If the boy disappears, they'd be doing me a favor.'

"'Then, we don't have an agreement?' asked Miss Sunset.

"'No, we don't,' said the uncle.

"Elijah was thrown into the sea. His skull lying on the sand fulfills the dream of those who pass through the world without leaving a trace.

"The liaison, after delivering the unwelcome news, asked them to take her to land before the personal sinking was completed. She made the entire journey standing with her back to the ship and her face to the sun. *Miss Sunset* was visible on the boat's stern as it carried her to the rocky coast."

The three players stood up and began to leave the room single file. I went with them, not understanding who had won the bet. And just like that, we're happy in Mumbai.

"Everything vanishes, but also endures," I told her as I passed by the woman of the third eye, who protected the entrance of the Fifth Library.

"The center is unmoving, and everything else," she whispered in my ear. "Stay. When you depart, don't forget to leave a new book."

# Book V: The Book of Contemporaries
# Fight Club

THE LABEL "GENERATION" IS a descriptor all authors almost certainly resist, as if it's a mark branded on them with a red-hot iron. But the fact remains that historical aptitudes exist and can produce differing responses from a similar origin, even if they don't leave identical markings. Not unlike what happens to laboratory animals.

In this circle, I tend to gather the collection of works by Cuban authors born in the second half of the '70s and the '80s, who lived during the crisis of the Special Period in Cuba, in a relative state of innocence. They witnessed the hardships and shortages, but accepted them as normal: a type of training that paralleled their own growth. They didn't wonder if writing would be a good future, they didn't experience publishers abandoning them, nor did they suffer a paper shortage, because they didn't write. They were unaware of some paradises, and if they did visit them, they accepted their demise without drama. Despite the decline of great celebrations, they responded willingly since they associated them with a stage of their lives they wanted to leave behind as they became adults. They don't belong—we don't belong—to a disillusioned generation, so they can't be rebellious or sentimental.

I'd like to draw attention to a trilogy of stories by this new writers' club. I discovered them in digital magazines and, with the exception of one that's already published, the others probably haven't made it to print yet and never will. I'm aware that appropriating their proposals basically demonstrates my personal preference and interest in revealing a certain deliberateness or a catalogue of nonconformities out of place in Cuban literature.

The narrator and protagonist of *The Color of Diluted Blood*, by Enrique Leich[1], who's heading toward the outskirts of Havana, comments "this is already pure periphery." A city, which years before had been the center of the world, is merely the suburbs to this adventurer. What stands out in this, as in other texts of similar situations, is the appropriation of a familiar international literary device that often uses cultural industry stars to satirize ways of life and modern society's perplexities, but in the Cuban reality this strategy acquires an offbeat flavor. That's what happens when you see Naomi Watts leaving El Vedado cinema, in one of Raúl Rosas's stories. Including celebrities in famous areas of the city converts the stories into almost fantasy-like experiences. In this way, what could possibly form a misappropriation ends up emphasizing the cracks in the national context.

*The Color of Diluted Blood* begins with an email written by the protagonist, who coincides with his author not only in the use of first person, but also in the authorship of a book (even though both share it with Stephen King), *I Was a Teenage*

---

1   I met Enrique Leich by chance. Leich is one of those writers who always seems out of reach. Even though he's right in front of you, you'll think you're lookisng at a photo in a magazine. He's practically mute, but has a nervous laugh that he abruptly mixes with profound comments. His laugh, by the way, can reproduce like a virus. One day, unexpectedly, in front of your family or friends, you pause in the middle of the merriment and say: "My goodness, that's not my laugh, that's Enrique Leich's." I probably managed to get close to him because we were both reading *2666*. Since we were the first ones to read it, we had no other choice except to talk with each other about the book. Little by little our phone conversations ended up lasting for hours. And yet, when we saw each other in person, we only exchanged a few short words. I'm not really sure how he does it, but his opinion seems to be the result of a consensus of numerous educated people. There's not a book he hasn't read or doesn't have an explanation for why he wouldn't like it. The last time I saw him he told me that not a single thing being written in Cuba at the time interested him, which meant that he didn't like anything I was writing either. I think that behind his laughter there's a very dangerous view of literature. I think the best way to move Cuban literature forward is to please Enrique Leich. If he doesn't like it, we're doomed.

*Grave Robber.* In his email to Christina Ricci, he asks her to visit his house in Havana, so he can take photographs of her to put on the cover of his next publication. After sending the message, our character picks up a power saw and heads toward a colonial-style house, a symbol he so helpfully uses to complete an image of transcendent national lineage. The battle, which in cinematic form would require a budget greater than the profits of three sugarcane harvests, we can enjoy in narrative form with all its extras and colors. (One of his colleagues brings a Hattori Hanzo sword, a gift from Uma Thurman when she posed for that accomplice's last book.) What comes next is nearly impossible to recount: an extraordinary crusade where our man's saw played the role that Robert Rodríguez, or preferably a lesser-known filmmaker, planned for it. Minutes before entering the traditional mansion, one of the players shows the others a map of the place, where he's outlined a strategy. The protagonist assures us it's a plan devised by his friend, who's never set foot inside. In other words, a band of writers carrying weapons prepares to attack an estate others might have called Tradition, which none of them are familiar with or care about. If the reality they encounter doesn't match the map, they can use their weapons arbitrarily and more extensively, which seems to be what happens.

The overlap of the two incompatible planes establishes a space of excessive writing, where the surprising discovery and failed expectations of both sides stand out. On one side a disregarded itinerary and on the other a desire to transition, which don't completely correspond.

One of these maps can be examined in digital publications, cartography that doesn't agree with the traditional publishing houses, but flourishes in the Inbox with random frequency and when least expected. I won't mention the ones I subscribe to and read more meticulously, so they can enjoy their anonymous celebrity a little longer and promote their secret existence.

One of them, where I found the first story, has a section called Guitar Shop. In each Guitar Shop, the publishing house 45rpm announces a list of works by young authors for the summer season. Surprisingly, the titles aren't fake. The only illusion this section retains for us is the parody of marketing. The classification rpm 01 is used for out-of-print titles. We don't know if these best sellers are impossible to obtain because an inordinate number of copies were sold or if they're literally out of print as their classification suggests.

The tendency toward an irrepressible production of such literature could indicate a new phase in the relationship between the author and his work within the Cuban context. An aloofness that's noticeably distant from the self-reflective approach. It gravitates closer to ephemeral variables, due more to exploitative contracts and a certain lack of interest in the perfection of writing, which is not so much an apparent lack of narrative rigor, but instead resembles unfinished, incomplete work, always left unedited. This way, it also creates new readers. Essentially, we are facing literature that doesn't allow re-reading. Not because of an exhausted supply, but almost the opposite: because there is always more, even if it's not summer season. When the time comes to establish hierarchies, this type of literature is elusive and suspicious of canonization. The result could verge on apolitical hedonism, a gesture of empty artifice, which could completely subvert literature's role. Sorry, *our* literature's role.

In any case, the friends have entered the colonial house and once inside they commence a new Cuban struggle against the demons. In one of the most sheltered rooms at the massacre's edge, they find a prominent Cuban writer of those days. The team has happened upon Ángel Escobar. But not just him. In the previously mentioned digital magazines, there's everything one would want to read for such entertainment, and which would take a while before reaching the publishing paths. Usurping the legitimate spaces occupied by others (represented by torrid rooms, contaminated by their overlapping bodies), evicting the inhabitants, and later discovering other forgotten authors while cleaning up, could redefine one of the missions assigned to the characters by the readers, who fight at a distance. However, the objective isn't to move into the house. After our protagonist cuts down the last royal palm tree in the house's interior patio with his power saw, the mission is completed and they leave. When he arrives home, Christina Ricci is waiting for him on the couch ready to be photographed, of course.

The grandfather who laments that they just don't write books like they used to would be absolutely right. The relationship between representation and national reality has been altered. As the title of Sylvia Molinos's[2] book, *Surfing between 500 Foreign Channels*, warns, the project consists of various program

---

2   We arranged to meet at a Café Literario that existed two years ago on 23 and 12. Sylvia Molinos had offered to show me why my first book of short stories was rubbish and was the last thing Cuban literature needed at that moment. I placed my book on the table, with strips of paper protruding from its pages as placeholders. I sensed I could see someone I knew on the other side of the window bars and I couldn't even say hello. Sylvia had promised to give me a Deleuzian criticism. It sounded like it could be entertaining. She read a story fragment in which the character was in the middle of a phone conversation. You could only hear what he was saying, never the person on the other end, an ex-girlfriend who was making him suffer. "The author has committed the great error of telephone conversations in a story," she warned me. Since I hadn't wanted the ex-girlfriend to talk, my hero's lines were questions based on what she'd just said to him, as if the character were deaf and the reader stupid. For example, if you assumed on the other end of the line she'd said: "I was at our old beach with my new boyfriend." My character, instead of saying: "How dare you take a stranger to the place we discovered together?" would cling to the telephone and say: "Are you saying you went to our beach with your new boyfriend?" That's what Sylvia called Utterly Ignoring the First Rule of Telephone Dialogues in Which You Hear Only One Character. Our table was quite close to a fly zapper and we could hear them burn up, or maybe it was the sound of a fatal short circuit. Sylvia Molinos noticed them and said the flies also saw the light at the end of the tunnel, but that didn't prove the existence of God. I believe she meant to say we're all wrong and the problem was the books.

fragments from a foreign television station. The mild sarcasm broadcasted by the headline is reminiscent of the famous national channels Six and Two. A direct allusion to plurality unfolds in the story, which is broken up into eight micro-stories on other screens, whose surfaces also reflect their own.

Arranged interviews, movies begun, surprise endings at the last minute by sheer coincidence, large crowds protesting harmoniously. This channel surfing also tunes in to surprising interruptions of daily life and between one jump and another it seems we've succeeded in recognizing some city corner, the face of a friend or someone famous. There's not always time to be certain. In the last fragment, a naked girl walks around, like an urgent muse, through a man's space, as he tries to avoid her. It's not really the final channel. We forget when the story began and when it ended. There are 500 possible ways to read this text. And maybe not even one of them is the program some character is seeking. How could he see them? Where did he direct the antenna? We sense something, a person is far away and the distance has caused him to wander between these other infinite realities.

*Surfing between 500 Foreign Channels* contemplates the uniqueness of depending more on the memorable search than on the stability of what is published. When this happens, the meddling narrator, a performer of sorts, takes hold of the story and presents it to the crowd he directly interacts with. Besides provoking and unbalancing the space occupied by the narrator and his listening audience, this also dissolves the performance limits his fiction proposes. He discovers a skeptical stance toward fiction's assumed norms and boundaries, a search for verisimilitude on other paths (suspicious of the usual drama of the well-constructed and better-told history), and a distancing from the narrative model that doesn't satisfy the authors' needs and expectations. Yes, quite a complicated rhizome.

A discovery highlighted by recognized, contemporary, cultural liberalness consists of text recycling, not always the classics (and not always belonging to the medium of literature). This process allows the authors to interact with references disinherited from their originality. Movie industry remakes, architectural revivals, and new arrangements of old songs now promote an approach to the rewritten text, but also the proliferation of readings that don't firmly belong to the original work, but to its replacement. For example, to read *Ulysses* before *The Odyssey*. Or "Eldorado," by Raúl Rosas,[3] before Raymond Carver's equivalent story, "Why Don't We Dance?"

In the story, "Eldorado," a couple walks around aimlessly until they arrive at an average city, where there's only one house with closed windows, but its front door is open. The furniture (bed, nightstands, dishwasher, television, video player, chairs, and sofa) are arranged on the grass in the yard, in a jumble suggesting a yard sale. Those who need electricity are still connected to cables buried under the grass leading to the house. The characters try out the furniture, like in children's fairy tales.

---

3    We usually met like two drug traffickers exchanging merchandise and later losing touch for a few months. The merchandise in question was some book Raúl Rosas brought with him, rarely his own, which he secretly borrowed from its true owner. Rosas engages in the dissemination of all books published outside of Cuba that fall into his hands. He always has at least three books with him and knows, without needing a written list, who is next in line for each book. He also lets you know what the upcoming books are. With his help, I was able to read *Mantra* by Rodrigo Fresán. When I told him I hadn't liked the book too much, he warned me that Fresán incorporated many musical references I was probably missing. "I miss the references too," he added, "but I know they're there, even though I don't see them." Raúl Rosas has a rather cryptic way of talking, as if he were thinking aloud or shooting at close range. That day we'd eaten hot dogs, exchanged books, and finished commenting on the reprint of an enjoyable novel by a Cuban author. I recommended it and told him no one would probably talk about it for eight years, but it was worth reading now, since it was very funny. We'd already left the place where we'd eaten and it was sunset. We went our separate ways at the corner of 14 and 21, near a carpentry shop, evident from the wood smell. "One thing I can promise you," said Rosas when it was time to say goodbye, "within eight years you and I'll be hilarious."

The woman climbs on the bed, while the man turns on the television. Later he enters the house and discovers the rooms are abandoned spaces with blank walls. In one room he finds a cadaver. He returns to the woman, who is watching a reality show, and tells her the house is empty. Later, as night falls, they lie down to sleep. They don't know if they'll stay there all their lives, or just one night. Nevertheless, a familiar, tragic tendency surrounds them, a certain unstable climate suggested in both cases by the television screen. The acceptance of the state of reality found by these characters, without questioning it, consists of a separation of mobile and immobile, tradition and proximity, and suspicion about a house with an open door and closed windows, all of which seem to require an inventory of routines in this narrative.

Supported by the casual progression of the story, the characters of "Eldorado" experience various stages. First, the encounter that directs them to the fantasy house. An exploration of land and a game of inherited roles within a conventional family takes place: the man goes out for food and clothes, the woman waits among the furniture watching television. Nonetheless, after discovering the cadaver in the empty rooms, the man returns to the woman and keeps his discovery from her. At this point the characters have returned to their larval state.

"I don't know what would be wonderful in these moments," says the man.

They reluctantly accept what they've found and their family doesn't prosper. In this calmness, there's a wish to drag out a moment, originating from a past experience and a mistrust of what the future holds. The great absence (supported by the finding of the patriarchal and anonymous cadaver), in addition to the distrust expressed by the television screen, like signals from a loyal subconscious, seals the couple's static and contradictory destiny. At the story's beginning, the woman said: "We'll always have those small things to remind us how big we could've been and never were." All these phrases of corrupt and repeated discourse belong to the past of the characters, who, as the story's progression shows, are nomads. If they carry something with them, they are small things, like a power saw.

In short, I believe I've read in these times and even in those that've most interested me, an overview of recurring behaviors in contemporary Cuban literature that could be simplified as the following. The places where the stories take place are dreamlike (even when they're filled with recognizable locations), a type of omnipresent unreality, as if the stories had a film-studio reference rather than a living context (or in this case writing studio). It's divested of all urban icons that could confirm the suggested narrative in a reading of short-sighted commitment. There's no inclusion of events in a national chronology. The mention of recent movies, television series, or current songs in the time period when the story was written, marks the time. An interest in the movie antidote and its most reoccurring topics leads to typical events of bad movies, classic scenes, and recycled dialogues in the stories. For example, a character enters a house and asks: "Hello! Is anyone here?" or in another the protagonist appears out of nowhere to save a friend who is losing a fight and they continue the battle together, after the friend thanks the protagonist. Additionally, there's a certain storyline hypersensitivity toward practiced narrations in video games, where the story is constructed in the instant when the hero decides which path to take in a network of possibilities. Undoubtedly we're in the presence of a discourse about identity, which sadly brings us closer to that rubric we avoid in principle: generation. Above the emptiness in which these stories and their adventures float, there exists a simultaneous erasing process, not as we expect, of some previous time (the past is a latent presence because of its recurrent omission and can fade away without the necessity of mediators), but rather the present itself.

Just before beginning the mentioned battle that'll move us toward failure, the players ask:

"Are we ready?"

"Of course not," they respond, "but what choice do we have."

\*

Before sunrise I walked into a gas station's tavern on the outskirts of El Paso. A woman polished the bar with a damp cloth, while another lined up chairs for the morning crowd. I chose a table beside the window. From there I could see the deserted highway and, if I turned my head a little, managed to distract myself watching the television suspended in a corner, showing the last part of *The Terminator*. No other customers arrived. Standing beside the full shelf of bottles, one woman told the other her recent dream:

"I dreamed I woke up in my house, as usual, and got everything ready to come in to work my shift. As I was opening the door, I remembered I'd left something in my bedroom. So I quickly went back, but when I was about to close the door, I remembered something else I'd forgotten and went back upstairs again. I repeated this many times, until at one point I paused in front of my bed and saw myself still sleeping. I realized I was dreaming and that's how I was able to wake up to get here on time."

"Something similar happened to me, but the opposite," said the other woman as she moved a chair. "When I opened the front door, I remembered I'd left something in the bedroom. I hesitated whether to go back or not, and I decided to leave it, so I'd arrive on time."

No other customers arrived. The sun didn't rise either.

"Maybe if you'd returned, you would've discovered you were sleeping soundly," joked the first woman.

"In that case, you wouldn't have woken up either and it's probably too late for both of us."

I supposed if the second woman were dreaming that I'd, consequently, be a small part of her dream. As would whichever of my predictions that belonged to the subconscious mind of the forty-year-old woman with messy hair and a weary laugh, who served rum all day and occasionally protested when a big rig blocked her view of the sunset while filling its tank. On the other hand, what was the elusive object both women forgot in their respective dreams?

On the TV, Sarah Connor reached an agreement with a Mexican kid to pay him four dollars for a Polaroid snapshot he'd taken of her. That photo, I recalled, is the one that the leader's father and future friend would see. For now the leader sleeps in amniotic fluid within his mother's round belly. She smiles while she caresses the parabola of her abdomen, as if she'd told herself and the baby:

"Everything vanishes, little one, but also endures."

All of a sudden, as if I were the one who'd awakened, the sky went dark. The bar was lit by neon lights and rumbled with the chords of Tejano music. Neither of the women was in the bar. An Indian demonstrated what a sober man can do, tossing a bottle and catching it behind his back. Then, tossing the bottle to the front again and making it spin before he served glasses he then slid down the bar toward the crowd. I realized the second woman had awakened in some room in the city and hadn't taken me with her.

The headlight reflections disappear into the wet highway. Fragile extremities of roaming monsters. White, red, and blue tentacles shattered the night's air, which was reserved for superheroes.

"Man, I like those little books with famous phrases," the taxi driver said as he looked for me in the rearview mirror. "I always try to memorize the phrases, so I can respond with them if passengers become talkative."

He maneuvered through the streets with a combination of routine and stress, as if he couldn't do anything else but move around Manhattan. Or as if he'd driven a spaceship for many years and now he'd spend the rest of his life stuck in a taxi.

"After I've driven a few blocks, I look at my passengers in the rearview mirror," he said looking at me. "And when we pass an image of one of my people on a billboard, I usually say: 'He must've done something bad or he wouldn't be so famous.' They always like it, without knowing it's a phrase from Robert Louis Stevenson. I don't really know who he is, but I do know he said that. My glovebox is full of little books with famous phrases. It's my portable library," he added, pointing to the little door beside the meters. "I figure if a police officer stops me, it'll take me awhile to find my papers in there. So, I know lots of phrases, too many. Oh yeah. And I use all of them, man. I rarely say something that hasn't already been said by some other guy. Many people like the phrases that have to do with God, but you have to know if they're in favor of God or not. Do you believe in God?"

I looked out the window as if I'd seen someone I knew and he seemed to accept that as my response.

"Sometimes I say: 'God is dead,' then I tell them it's a phrase from Nietzsche that summarizes the crisis of modern, European thought. You learn information when some little books have comments written in them, man, but others don't and that's bad because, well, let's suppose you like how a phrase sounds, but you don't know when to use it or whom to pass it on to. If I say that one from Nietzsche and I see they don't accept it, then I say one by Einstein, who's more famous here: 'God doesn't play dice.' With this Albert Einstein explains that nothing is left to fate, which is difficult for a taxi driver to accept, but I use it just the same. There's another one about God, which is a little more complex: 'The very impossibility in which I find myself to prove that God is not, discloses to me his existence.' That's from La Bruyère. 'Cynicism is pure, intellectual dandyism.' Now that unites two points of ignorance, because I don't know who George Meredith is, nor do I understand the phrase, but I use it, man, when I drive near Washington Square, and it always works well. Another one I like, but don't know how to use, is from René Descartes: 'Bad books engender bad habits and bad habits engender good books.' Camus: 'Myths have more power than reality. The Revolution as myth is the definitive revolution.' This last one I say almost always when I don't have passengers. When there's a traffic jam at noon and no one's moving, then I usually say: 'When, O Catiline, do you mean to cease abusing our patience?' It's the historic phrase Cicero used in the senate to denounce the plot devised by Catiline and the popular party to gain access to power by force. Thanks to those words he was able to reveal himself to the conspirators and prevent the plan from taking place. 'It's better to know useless things than to know nothing.' Seneca. 'If my right hand knew what my left hand was doing, it'd cut it off.' That's what the king said to the Pope's envoy, who asked him why he was preparing his navy forces, which caused Italy's distrust. I almost always say that when I drive around Ground Zero. At Christmas or when I see the sidewalks full of people, I say: 'He who pursues two things at once, doesn't reach one and lets the other go.' Benjamin

Franklin. In the morning when the buildings obstruct the day's first light and the city lies in limbo, I tend to say: 'We know what we are, but we don't know what we can be.' That's from William Shakespeare, the same guy who gave us 'to be or not to be,' Prince Hamlet's famous phrase that summarizes an eternal contradiction. When a passenger who's just arrived in this country gets in, which is something that never gets by me, man, I tell him something he doesn't follow at all: 'You too, my son?' which was what the Roman emperor Julius Caesar said when he defended himself from his enemies' attack and saw Brutus with a dagger in his hand, ready to attack him. But, of course, I use it in another way. If a model gets into my taxi when I'm in front of Seagram or the LVMH tower, I usually say: 'Do you come from Heaven or rise from the abyss, Beauty?' A verse from the universal symbolist poet Baudelaire, who used it to express ambivalence about the concept of beauty, very common here in this mental state. When flying through Times Square at night: 'Time is gold.' Do you think we Americans invented that? Well, no, we've only improvised it in a few good movies. The phrase is from Theophrastus of Lesbos, Aristotle's disciple who wrote about man and plants. What I told you about the good movies has its flaws, because lately I like TV series better."

Before leaving his taxi, I asked the driver to choose a famous phrase for our journey. He turned around and said: "It's one from Piet Mondrian, man. He was a painter. Even painters have famous phrases. In the artist's opinion, art consists of expressing universal harmony, excluding all arbitrariness. You can see it in his work as he looks for balance between form and color. Equilibrium this zombie life lacks. The phrase is coming, man: 'Art will disappear as life becomes more balanced.'"

In Wellington one night I found myself in a bar, where men resembling sailors were drinking enormous glasses of beer and shouting at a woman dressed in blue, who was waiting on them. Her name was Molly Blue and at midnight, upon the request of several sailors and by her own desire, barely concealed by her smile, she stood up on a table to sing a ballad.

Looking at her it seemed natural to me that New Zealand had produced one writer famous for her short stories and another for her detective novels. I watched with special interest the way Molly Blue embraced the men, with her arms crossed while she sang, as if to support herself and give them pleasure.

> *the life of jim johnson was long and happy*
> *like mine and like yours, like the life of my love*
> *jim johnson who's not the same as in the song.*

> *jim johnson wrote a novel in the woods,*
> *surviving on squirrels*
> *and an outrageous number*
> *of preserved peaches.*
> *drunk men read it and ran*
> *to ask forgiveness of their children.*

> *jim johnson's life was orderly and happy*
> *like yours and mine, like that of my love*
> *jim johnson who's not the same as in the song.*

> *at Christmas the sheriff wanted everyone at his house.*
> *jim decided to misplace the address*
> *throwing smooth stones into the river.*

*his pants were dripping when they hung him.*
*molly blue went to see him swing*
*and jim winked at her.*

*jim johnson's life was orderly and happy*
*like yours and mine, like that of my love*
*jim johnson who's not the same as in the song.*

The sailors yelled the chorus and then took turns adding a new verse. Singing along with them was easy. With their beards wetted with beer, the men sang verses full of patriotic pride and were pleased with each new interjection, which they received as if it were a long-lost letter. *jim johnson was a pirate for a while / he crushed ships and climbed masts.* One of them stopped in the middle of his rhyme and the rest kicked him out. Until then I'd hidden in the crowd, but the order of singers followed a line of the person beside you, and he was only one away from me. Making her way through the crowd, Molly Blue served me a pitcher of beer and on top of it floated a dirty little piece of paper where she'd copied the verse I then sang.

*jim johnson was a pirate for a while,*
*he crushed ships and climbed masts.*
*a fortune-teller begged him*
*that he do it no more.*
*his ship floated adrift a couple years,*
*until it crashed into America.*

The crowd applauded my addition. They slapped me on the back and clinked their empty pitchers against my lucky one. I looked at Molly to thank her, but she concealed our collaboration so well that she ignored me the entire night.

One of the sailors began to tell me the story of a woman he'd met whose vagina had grown a tooth.

"After several months without having sex," the sailor told me, "Hilda discovered that her vagina had grown a tooth. She was scared and quickly moved her fingers away from the hard, angular growth her flesh had produced. It didn't cause her any pain or trouble other than the surprise of being an absurd manifestation. She didn't mention it to anyone. She figured it'd vanish the same way it'd developed. When little by little an entire set of baby teeth appeared, she was convinced it was, without doubt, a natural phenomenon and biologically correct. One morning while she was eating breakfast, Hilda decided to feed it. She took a piece of bread and, after she chewed it up to soften it with her saliva, she brought it close to the other mouth, which devoured the snack effortlessly. From that moment she started feeding it with maternal devotion. This led them both to early mornings when the vagina woke her with pains that didn't stop until it'd consumed a full bottle of warm milk, or to rainy afternoons sheltered by half-open windows, when they shared a Swiss chocolate bar. The vagina gained weight, became a rosy melon color, and sometimes smiled, showing its perfect teeth. Apparently one Monday, the vagina talked. 'Hilda' was the first word Hilda heard come from that part of her body, and she was so happy with the progress that she started an energetic phonetic program and the vagina quickly achieved perfect diction. It tried to make amends for its late arrival and asked about everything. Hilda accommodated it by telling about her life before it appeared and they talked for hours. They fell asleep telling each other about their failures and hopes. Soon after, Hilda started to be more careful in her posture, so as not to harm it or make conversation difficult. She reduced seat cushion pressure, claustrophobic underwear, and baths that submerged it mercilessly in the tub. Consequently, her democratic arrangement led her to positions that were more horizontal. Even when walking, the vagina demanded more benevolent positions that didn't affect its equilibrium. Hilda, delighted with her alter ego's increasing determination, willingly accepted the movements that looked more like those of a crab or horrifying animal than a person. Over time her arms and legs became four homogeneous appendages, while the vagina, by this time free from the oppression of the thighs, expanded and Hilda's head tried to figure out how to rest the stiffness of her neck between what used to be her arms. She scurried about the house like a spider, and when she needed to reach the table or a window, she did it indistinctly with any two of her extremities. They spoke less, since now they were absolutely different as night and day, and yet the synchronism of their actions ensured, without the need for words, an understanding, a certain satisfied harmony. The vagina, for its part, emulated the carrying out of all tasks, while Hilda gave up, surprised to see it advance with more and more abilities. The vagina began to do everything and to spend more time upright, while the head was pressed between strengthened appendages now resembling her weak thighs. The glutes lowered and the breasts looked for a higher place. It became difficult for Hilda to say anything, even more so to attempt to return to her normal position since her legs had become like delicate hands. The vagina, for her part, repeated Hilda's own stories to her as if it were she and not Hilda who had been the protagonist of the events. One morning the vagina got up, filled the bathtub, and got in determinedly. Hilda awoke frightened by the bang of her head against the pearl-colored bottom of the tub and attempted to bury herself in her own body, closing the thighs so the water wouldn't follow her inside. The vagina finished her bath, dried off her skin, and dolled herself up in front of the mirror. Even though she didn't like any of the clothes she found in the closet, she settled on an outfit that seemed the least disagreeable to her and went out onto the street. When she came across the first person she didn't know, she showed them all her teeth.

"This story," said the sailor, "the vagina told me. I never saw

Hilda."

Everything vanishes, but also endures, I thought. Before leaving the bar, with the bodies collapsed on the tables and the overturned chairs, I approached Molly Blue, who was asleep on the bar. She awkwardly moved one finger to my lips, as if in her drunken state she couldn't judge the proper distance, and said:

"Tell me something that'll scare me. The scary stories always help me lose my fear."

"Years ago," I told her through her finger, "I was hitchhiking on the highway and sat under a bridge with a garlic vendor, who seemed to have no better way to pass the time than to share advice about literature. You know, Molly Blue, it was almost nighttime, with a psychedelic orange sky, dry gusts that'd split your lips, and you're willing to bet you'd die that afternoon, or that you're the only survivor on the planet. You and the garlic vendor. The vendor said:

"'Offend your public. Those who feel offended will offer double commentaries before leaving, they're dregs. Those who accept the offense, believe it, and sense you judge them, they're also dregs. There'll be one who feels sorry for you. He's your audience. Never write reviews or submit articles to magazines, avoid reading in public and knowing your contemporaries.' The last part I remember in particular because, maybe looking for a comfortable position in which to listen, I'd looked down at the garlic braids with their domestic and macabre perfection, just like what you're thinking now, like destiny."

As I helped her lift the bar section to allow me to pass through, I heard her say:

"That one, who's collapsed like all the others, is the Librarian, my husband. I don't mind that you stay, but you should promise to leave a book before you leave."

"I don't bring anything with me except blurred memories of my past and exhaustion from days without sleep."

"Weariness will prevent you from seeing if you are already

asleep or if you still come here nervous about the wolves voicing their apathy. It's better to forget the memories of the past, they'll return without you calling for them. You'll have to write something inside. Go ahead."

# Book VI: The Book of Fame
## Lost in Translation

HE LIKED BOB DYLAN, even though he referred to him as Bobo Dylan. Japanese speakers don't end on the last consonant, but instead add a vowel without thinking about the consequences. We were listening to "I Want You," which I consider a really bittersweet song; sadness in its most primitive state. The colorful lights jumped into the car and as I sat in there I was almost pleased I'd been run over. That's how our short friendship started. My first night in Tokyo and I've already been rammed into, I thought.

The taxi driver had picked me up off the street while he uttered something I didn't understand, although it was easy to guess it was something about paying attention to the buildings' lights, that a car wouldn't fly out of them, I should've been looking down, and that's what happens to me because I'm foreign and think that everything in Japan is like a medieval-themed anime. I kept saying, "Gomenasai." In just a few hours, I'd been so contaminated by the Japanese effervescence that I was asking forgiveness for causing a car to make me fly five meters in the air. On top of it all, my *I'm sorry* was rather samurai-like, choppy and full of pain, which was totally justified since my right wrist hurt as if it'd been cut open with a knife to stick a piece of ice inside it. The taxi driver watched me from behind his bangs that brushed against his eyelashes. I assumed his hairstyle also had something to do with the accident. As if he had three focal points, the driver looked forward, then craned his neck to see how the street disappeared in the rearview mirror, and lastly turned to look at me. With my good hand, I held my throbbing arm. I smiled imagining myself forgotten on the seat. The taxi driver also smiled, trying to respond the same way, but he ended up producing a look that clearly showed he didn't understand anything, much less the motive of my agreeableness.

"Welcome to Tokyo," he said. "My name is Ryo."

His facial expression reminded me of an archway anchored in an Eastern lake in the middle of two spaces, identical due to their boundlessness, where nonetheless, something similar to Benjamin's diminishing aura changes as one crosses it. When two strangers seek a third language to communicate, the result resembles a collection of common interests. After two stoplights, Ryo San and I discover we share the same passion for a certain anime where the warriors possess a spirit weapon that elevates them to a state of greater power, exhibited in the development of their swords. The weapon's properties vary according to the warrior and are invoked by a word spoken in the most arduous moment of the fight, when they're tired of training and decide to invoke their true abilities. The word is *bankai*. For example, once uttered the sword might transform into six thousand small reflections that penetrate the adversary's skin, draining his blood, or into a serpent of rings that separate like coins. There are warriors who succeed in building a cathedral in which there's no light, where the shadows are abrasive and the adversary dies on his knees. Ryo San confessed that in his free time he was an incorrigible reader. That shared obsession had motivated both of us, far apart and unknown to each other, to come up with the same idea: to envision the *bankai* of writers.

He'd imagined ones for Japanese writers, of which I only recognized Murakami, and the version of his *bankai* was very close to one I'd never considered. I'd invented Lezama's *bankai*. Anyone who dared to fight him ended up exhausted. Ryo San didn't know him. I doubted his book *Paradiso* existed in Japanese script. I pondered a translation into English, but it didn't seem possible. We agreed no one would ever know which warrior was the most powerful. I told him maybe this particular author's *bankai* was as if our glazed avenue were the opposite of a Havana patio, where it was possible to hear moss growing and through his spinal nerves to return to the middle of this street to find it empty, submerged in water with an occasional flying fish jumping and square-shaped ripples repeating from the primordial patio. Ryo San thought it was a magnificent perimeter for the battle.

We were quiet for a while, for a few blocks. Then we started talking about the universal *bankai*, not just the Japanese or Cuban ones.

Victor Hugo's is a beast formed from brick arches, like a Roman aqueduct that on one end adopts the head of a girl and on the other a bat. Poe's is a tree at twilight, with an epitaph written in each leaf and its lowest branch waits for a raven. Hemingway's is a water buffalo from the Caribbean Sea on whose back sits a killer fish and a lonely, deaf woman. Bukowski's is a typewriter abandoned in a ditch full of rainwater, carrying along with it weeds, obscene napkins, and mutilated dolls. Thomas Mann's is a parachutist hanging from a gigantic tree, where he agonizes and understands existence through a vision of an amber-colored leaf. Onetti's is an empty bar with a line of beds turned over in the shape of a heart, divided by paper walls and in any one of them an adolescent boy waits, wielding a paddle. Bolaño's is himself, Roberto walking toward his opponent, passing through him with his head down as if the other were a ghost that our warrior couldn't see. Chekhov's is a lethal snowflake resting on a strawberry leaf. Dostoyevsky's is a prison cell where the opponent watches St. Petersburg pass by as if it were a boat and then kisses the ground, begging for mercy in the form of a revolver without bullets. Raymond Chandler's is a Chevrolet without lights going full speed through the streets of Havana and Pasadena simultaneously without knowing which city he's in.

When we arrived at the hospital, it shone like an electric elephant or the deployment of a surgeon's powerful sword. Ryo San translated the doctor's evaluation about my x-ray. A bone in my wrist had a fracture and I should use a plastic splint secured with a bandage. It sounded good to me. At least it wasn't a cast.

On the way back, after other stoplights, we found out that in addition to Bobo Dylan and the convertible anime swords, we also liked the series *Lost*. According to Ryo San's summary, *Lost* is the story of some characters trapped on an island, who spend the whole time looking for the way to return home, but don't have a home to return to. Then he said it was beautiful. Since he said that in one of the intervals when he looked at the axis of the street, I thought he might be referring to something else and that I was simply nostalgic.

Finally, after the subject of *Lost*, maybe energized by the proximity and continuity of titles, we got to the story Ryo San had reserved for that night. I believed it was a secret he dared to share after our mental battles. In other words, he was tired of training and had decided to show his true skills. To liberate his *bankai*. My bilingual, brakeless taxi driver had acted in *Lost in Translation*, the movie directed by Sofia Coppola in 2003, in which Charlotte, played by Scarlett Johansson, stays with her husband at a Tokyo hotel, where she meets an American actor named Bob Harris, played by Bill Murray.

The title translates to Spanish as *Perdidos en Tokio* (*Lost in Tokyo*) and, according to Ryo San, in his country it was publicized as *Lost without Reason*. Even though the Japanese title indicated a certain untranslatable play on words, the end result didn't fit the sense of the film. It was definitely lost in translation.

His appearance for posterity occurred in the scene in which Charlotte and Bob Harris arrive at a Japanese man's house, where there's a small gathering of friends. Ryo San was one of the party guests, which of course doesn't end where the movie tells it, but rather the morning of the next day. The last American to leave was Scarlett. They ended up leaning on the glass, the karaoke continued playing songs, but no one felt like singing. Once in a while someone mumbled a verse like a zombie that couldn't help itself and its mouth spoke alone.

"That happens after smoking so much and partying all night," Ryo San warned me, in case I didn't know. "The mouth takes on a certain determination and ends up letting senseless phrases escape or at the least with a feeling that doesn't always have any meaning and is merely a lip exercise or an unconditional reflex to tune the vocal chords. Maybe that's why she said what she said, as if we couldn't understand her, in reality few could hear her, and those who understood English were even fewer, but I listened carefully to her," explained Ryo San. And I listened to him.

"She had already taken off the pink wig she was using. She'd hung it on one of her knees and brushed it like a faceless princess. I remember thinking constantly that at any moment the glass would break and we'd fall into the street, but I didn't have the strength to sit up and the idea made me laugh. Scarlett said she didn't like certain jokes from the movie that made fun of not knowing the language of the foreign city. She said that ultimately the same things happen in English. There are jokes about the lack of communication, and even though you understand the complete phrase, you don't grasp the true meaning or the intention of the person who said it. She added that she'd prefer to film another *Ghostbusters* with Bill Murray than be tied to the screenplay at those Japanese hours. Bill Murray was marvelous, as was the film crew. She trusted the beauty of the film and the loneliness of the two characters. The fault was completely hers, Scarlett Johansson's, who had the name of a heroine of a national novel and a physique that, according to the makeup artists, could compete with Marilyn Monroe or Grace Kelly, even Lauren Bacall when she was nineteen years old. And Jean Harlow too. Where she came closest to her character Charlotte was when she said that all the girls, when they're looking for something to be good at, they go through a photographer phase. She started crying and insisted, laughing, that it was the biggest truth she'd seen written on paper and she doubted she'd find another thing like that the rest of her life. She'd already passed her photographer phase. She'd photographed dried leaves from Central Park's trees, stairs of her building, subway graffiti, steamy windows in Brooklyn, and newspaper-reading beggars. All that'd been just before she turned entirely to acting, despite the fact that even as a girl she knew she'd be an actress and attended several schools for talented young people. She always was a little afraid of that moment, and it'd arrived with this movie in Tokyo. She knew it with every new scene they filmed. In the future, she'd have to disguise herself so she wouldn't be recognized everywhere. Her naked photographs would be worth more than a drawing of Edward Hopper, she wouldn't be able to take off her clothes at the beach, and her sexual encounters would have to be more protected than when she was fifteen. She'd have to forget forever homemade pornography, so naïve and sometimes too honest. She'd even have to stop karaoke, because someone could record her improvisations.

"'Even now I won't go to the Pearl River market or the stores on the Lower East Side,'" Ryo San told me she'd said, "'or to see the penguins in Central Park. I'll confess to the magazines that I read Truman Capote and that my favorite movie is *Charlie and the Chocolate Factory*. I'll make advertisements for Calvin Klein perfumes and Louis Vuitton. I'll pose for L'Oreal and Reebok. My photos will appear and they'll be accompanied by blocks of notes, such as: crepe dress by Marc Jacobs, gold earrings by Temple St. Clair, silver necklace by Me&Ro, as if it were an illustration in an anatomy book. And they'll lie, oh how they'll lie! They'll publish, for example, that one of my phobias is cockroaches. But in reality, I could adopt a newly hatched cockroach and keep it company until its last day without the least repulsion. They'll report I've had my nose done or had silicone injected in my lips. For my part, I'll also say foolish things, sometimes without meaning to, unguarded thoughts.

And yet other things I'll say out of plain maliciousness, so they can confirm that movie stars are daft, and, in those situations I won't offend myself, rather I'll offend the magazines, publicity, and the comedy of errors. I'll carry around a grumpy Chihuahua and announce my favorite food is Lombardi's veggie pizza and a Diet Coke or a piece of key lime pie, preferably homemade.'

"She said that not being aware of it or simply acting as if nothing were happening was the fastest way to the snob oasis in which so many others, whom she wouldn't mention, were already floating," explained Ryo San. "She'd have to become a specialist who dedicates herself to stealing the same jewel every day, every minute of her life. And that jewel she'd have to remove cautiously was none other than her own life, the spontaneity of what could've been her existence. From that moment death would accompany her like a Siamese twin sister and alongside it the fear of dealing with it, as if she were leaving something incomplete, something that, nevertheless, couldn't remain unfinished and whose cosmic outcome cost her all her time, and that talent of posterity was precisely what the Siamese sister seemed to pursue and desire. From that moment onward, she'd be living her life like a candle in the wind. With great directors, she'd film historical dramas, film noir, magical stories, and perfect comedies, one after another, traveling in the front seat of a rollercoaster. She saw it all clearly as if she'd already signed all the contracts of her whole career. She said she sensed like a snake the moment she'd have a house in Los Angeles, and the snakebite would hurt tremendously because you don't have to live in California to know what life is like there. And, on top of it all, the same thing was happening to her character Charlotte. She'd moved to Los Angeles after getting married and just thinking about it made her miss Manhattan. Someone got up, boiled water for tea, and then served it with the enthusiasm of a sleepwalker. She said thank you and added that Manhattan was like a man sitting on a bench, who knows all the rules of seduction, and that the other, California, was the same man, blond and a little younger, who knew the same rules, but without a hint of seduction. She tried the tea and cursed because it burned her lips. Later she smiled a little and dried the tears that ran down her face as if they were fake. She confessed she'd had to film a simple scene three times in which she had to walk across a pedestrian crossing at the exit of Hachiko, where she watched a thirty-meter-long dinosaur walk by on a building's screen and later a procession of elephants returning to the city. She had to repeat the scene, because her eyes kept filling with tears she couldn't control, as she grasped her transparent umbrella. Sofia approached her and asked her to save the emotion for the final scenes, because she thought she was inside the character of Charlotte.

"'But I wasn't acting at all,'" she'd told Ryo San. "'It seemed like I was walking alone again in Times Square, I wasn't recognized, and that's something that'll never happen to me again. At that moment, I was an extinct animal, but I controlled myself because a talented girl can't just dedicate herself to taking mediocre snapshots. I crossed the crosswalk surrounded by Japanese people my size. One hundred seventy centimeters tall.'

"She dried her cheeks again with the palm of her hand," he continued, "and put the pink wig on again. She looked for herself in the cloudy reflection that faded in the window as day rose, adjusted her bangs, and left after enthusiastically saying goodbye to everyone."

Ryo San didn't ask where he should take me. For some reason that certain Asian logic follows, he's returned me to the place of the accident and stopped there as if the trip had ended. I thanked him and he bowed his head. As a final point, he asks if we can imagine together what Bobo Dylan's *bankai* would be. We conclude his would be a skyscraper with a blond woman seated behind the glass of the highest floor, looking at the silent city and humming a melody, "like a complete unknown, like a rolling stone." Ryo San says goodbye with a "*bankai!*" I believe the splint on my injured wrist provides credibility as a warrior, but my image will change tomorrow when I have to sign autographs at the presentation of my first book translated into all the world's languages. Getting out of the taxi, I respond: "*Bankai!*" From the sidewalk, two Japanese women, walking by arm in arm, smile, I assume at me.

\*

With their backs to the ruins of an old university, three old women sat knitting and selling their handiwork. A hat, a scarf, a map of a historic city, and two gloves that should probably be the same size, but weren't. They used decorative pieces rescued from the rubble to hold down the corners of the cloth where they displayed their goods. A scrolled bracket, the corner of a column's capital, a section of a gargoyle's face with only one eye and its lips extended as if blowing away the clouds.

"Everything vanishes, but also endures," I told them, looking at the reclaimed debris.

The oldest smiled, nostalgic or disappointed by the lack of sales, and responded:

"When touring a Library or any other space organized by man, the time variable reemerges, but this time through a basic inability to appreciate the collection as a whole. Therefore, it's necessary that the traveler know every aspect. The tour will result in a euphemism for the impossibility of being omnipresent and reaffirms his soothing character in the arc's end. The wandering ends when we arrive at the same point where we began. With this memorable figure in space, the willingness to feign that nothing has happened is affirmed."

Without leaving her knitting, another of the women said:

"Man is an animal that has forged a certain sensibility from the gathering of his impossibilities, which he has called experience. The journey has been enhanced and has evolved into a profitable one. In the end, space is an impossibility for humans. Without the thread of time, it's a figment of one's imagination to walk through the Library, because the Library itself is impossible. Now we can begin to call space: absolute time."

Turning her head toward the landscape of ruins, the third and smallest woman added:

"If the past century devoted its literature to the exploration of time, then it would appear the literature of this century has chosen the search for space."

The other two looked at her as if she'd committed an indiscretion.

"And you? Do you also seek a Library? The last one?"

I nodded my head affirmatively.

"And most certainly you began with a search for a celestial woman, you've encountered taxi drivers, waitresses, snake charmers, idle men, sailors, criminals, pessimistic beggars, jealous Librarians, talking animals, and precocious girls. The same old story."

"Yes."

"And what have you written?"

I thought to myself: a story about the loss of innocence and the origins of writing. A story of magic regarding emigration and transcendence. A variation of a particular Russian melody with suicides and imperfect gunshots. The memories of a father who has sent his son to a beast. The adventures and misfortunes of my contemporaries. The perplexity of a suddenly famous author lost in a large city. The same old story.

Without letting me respond, the smallest woman asked: "And what relationship is there between what you've written and what you've lived?"

"They're not questions for you to answer," they said as in unison. "We'll present you with a predictable puzzle. If you answer it correctly, we'll allow you to pass."

Their voices began to overlap, sometimes coinciding and other instances chasing each other, one word pursuing another and then a third, all perfectly identical.

"While she was weaving in the early morning hours in Ithaca, Penelope was visited by three apparitions. A slave, whom she'd never seen before and would never see again, entered her estate, looked at her a long time, and then mumbled: 'Odysseus has died, abandon the weaving.' What did the second and third say? And how did Penelope respond?"

Under a gray sky, the ruins resembled desert sand dunes. I reviewed my journey up until this point. I was only missing one Library. Perceiving the idea of incompleteness and eternal memory as polar opposites of the mission, I answered:

"The second arrived as a young androgynous man who stated callously: 'You have also died. You were never born. You rot below the tree on a Spartan hillside on a cloudy afternoon. Your body ferments in the ground of a land you never abandoned, and nothing has come of the time you dedicated to a warrior who disappointed the gods. The men court you like an empty dress, which is convenient for them since it doesn't say yes or no. You could walk among them naked like a wayward wolf and they'd see nothing more than withered skin and fingers made long and trembling from weaving. Penelope doesn't exist, abandon the weaving.'"

They smiled the same nervous laughter, while they looked at one another and agreed.

Encouraged, I continued: "The third apparition appeared as a spider hanging from a roof beam and screamed: 'You have ignored two warnings. In the first I disclosed to you that the man you were waiting for was dead and, as such, the cloth you extend in reverse on your thighs has no meaning. Even so, you unwound the thread and continued your needle's efforts. I returned and revealed to you that you were dead; not only because of the faith you maintain, but rather in a more abstract sense and one no less certain, of that other waiting that carries you to the end of your days. None of this made you burn the cloth. Today I come to proclaim the shroud you weave will survive you twice over, beyond you and Telemachus's descendants, and also the gods who delayed the arrival of an incognito swineherd, who will be your husband. Why then do you not rest your hands and leave such vigilance out of man's world?'"

The three women agreed again, silently this time.

"And what did she answer?" the youngest one asked.

"I don't know."

They laughed scandalously and then responded in unison:

"You've answered correctly, stranger. Penelope said: 'I don't know. I can't know that.'"

I found the Seventh Library empty. (If the last pages of my journey appear blank, even without the beneficial numbers on the pages—three, five, six empty pages would suffice to bear witness to my last discovery. However, the paper's whiteness could possibly disseminate doubt about the noble typing errors, or maybe I should say of pixelation. Held up to a backlight, these are deserted pages, in the same way that we demand a word to name the void.)

Walls offering scant shade enabled me to admire a pristine space, seen for the first time. My journey left so few signs of my presence that I began to suspect previous visits. Hollow rectangles in which I could confirm the walls' thickness that revealed other wide corridors, and just as deserted. Narrow pathways crossed one another in the air, projecting an anonymous shadow. I was here before. I'm still here. Simultaneously I wander the chambers without running into myself. Time doesn't exist if there are no written texts by men who will disappear with time's passing, nor is there in all the chambers of this Library a Librarian other than me. Here I'll be able to rest without another story hindering me.

I figured it wasn't necessary to write a single word more. The world and its illusion of posterity didn't require another work. I loathed the texts I'd written in a state of presumed lucidity, of abomination. In one of the pavilions, I encountered a white toad, but it didn't speak to me. It jumped twice and was lost in the whiteness without textures of a perspective plane.

Since then, I've amused myself scratching two short phrases in the frame of an inside window, in a hypnotic circular inclination, as if I'd borrowed them and was now returning them. *The center is unmoving, but miniscule. Everything vanishes, but also endures.*

When I finish, it seems I'm reading these words for the first time. One can write literature out of obligation or regret or apathy. For fear of death. For money, assuming literature is a road to a life of luxury, a seemingly baseless argument. One can also write for entertainment, for misanthropy, for childhood yearning, or for competition with contemporary writers or others long since dead, who still create literature. Out of such a ridiculous perception of life that produces pity or encouragement. To prove something, for example, as in this case, that the text were a trigonometric reflection. To believe there's a good path and that only the one who writes can see it. Or to believe there's no such good path and only the one who writes can attest to its non-existence. To spend a night in the Seven Libraries of the World. But, regardless of the reasons, which are fewer than those suggested here, literature will always be written to explore a communication with an unknown and familiar abyss, one we possibly call patiently, or absurdly, the reader. And in each case, to tell him what? Something that pretends to be insignificant, and yet is everything. In order to let him know someone is here, thinking about exactly that. Like a scream returned as an echo. If that echo could last just a little longer, which is asking a lot. If it could be published, stowed away in a cavern reverberating until another solitary visitor arrives. And, if that visitor were you (and it has to be you otherwise this couldn't be) and you listen to it, we wouldn't be so alone. Even though the echo isn't anyone, it's an absence that announces itself.

I didn't find out if my reflection saved some relevance for the world, but for me it did. And I didn't find out if that *for me* held some relevance for the world, but I believe it should have. I didn't feel obliged to write another book to spend the night there, because there was no night nor sleeplessness. Even so, I wrote one more. I left it suspended in the air, the edge of the pages brushing up against the closest wall.

I'd like to justify myself like this: In the third night I spent there, among the purity and chaos of an absolute labyrinth, I began to write. Indeed, night and intermediary are impossible. There's no other time than the tapestry of time, but light and whiteness announce a primal source that will consequently deliver the conclusion to its rightful place. I believe glimpsing this led me to write the last book in the Seventh Library. I believe writing the last book enabled me to remain in the library for all time. And you, with me.

*

# Book VII: The Book of the Book
# The Last Librarian

Born in Cuba in 1981, OSDANY MORALES holds an MFA in Creative Writing from New York University. The author of several novels and story collections, he has received the David Award for short fiction, the International Prize for Fiction Casa de Teatro and the Alejo Carpentier Award.

KRISTINA L. BONSAGER (1970) is from the United States and has extensive experience in Argentina and Denmark. With an MA and PhD in Hispanic Literature, she has worked as a Spanish professor and translator. This is her second book translation, first in English.

MICHAL AJVAZ, *The Golden Age.*
*The Other City.*
PIERRE ALBERT-BIROT, *Grabinoulor.*
YUZ ALESHKOVSKY, *Kangaroo.*
FELIPE ALFAU, *Chromos.*
*Locos.*
JOE AMATO, *Samuel Taylor's Last Night.*
IVAN ÂNGELO, *The Celebration.*
*The Tower of Glass.*
ANTÓNIO LOBO ANTUNES, *Knowledge of Hell.*
*The Splendor of Portugal.*
ALAIN ARIAS-MISSON, *Theatre of Incest.*
JOHN ASHBERY & JAMES SCHUYLER, *A Nest of Ninnies.*
ROBERT ASHLEY, *Perfect Lives.*
GABRIELA AVIGUR-ROTEM, *Heatwave and Crazy Birds.*
DJUNA BARNES, *Ladies Almanack.*
*Ryder.*
JOHN BARTH, *Letters.*
*Sabbatical.*
DONALD BARTHELME, *The King.*
*Paradise.*
SVETISLAV BASARA, *Chinese Letter.*
MIQUEL BAUÇÀ, *The Siege in the Room.*
RENÉ BELLETTO, *Dying.*
MAREK BIENCZYK, *Transparency.*
ANDREI BITOV, *Pushkin House.*
ANDREJ BLATNIK, *You Do Understand.*
*Law of Desire.*
LOUIS PAUL BOON, *Chapel Road.*
*My Little War.*
*Summer in Termuren.*
ROGER BOYLAN, *Killoyle.*
IGNÁCIO DE LOYOLA BRANDÃO, *Anonymous Celebrity.*
*Zero.*
BONNIE BREMSER, *Troia: Mexican Memoirs.*
CHRISTINE BROOKE-ROSE, *Amalgamemnon.*
BRIGID BROPHY, *In Transit.*
*The Prancing Novelist.*

GERALD L. BRUNS, *Modern Poetry and the Idea of Language.*
GABRIELLE BURTON, *Heartbreak Hotel.*
MICHEL BUTOR, *Degrees.*
*Mobile.*
G. CABRERA INFANTE, *Infante's Inferno.*
*Three Trapped Tigers.*
JULIETA CAMPOS, *The Fear of Losing Eurydice.*
ANNE CARSON, *Eros the Bittersweet.*
ORLY CASTEL-BLOOM, *Dolly City.*
LOUIS-FERDINAND CÉLINE, *North.*
*Conversations with Professor Y.*
*London Bridge.*
MARIE CHAIX, *The Laurels of Lake Constance.*
HUGO CHARTERIS, *The Tide Is Right.*
ERIC CHEVILLARD, *Demolishing Nisard.*
*The Author and Me.*
MARC CHOLODENKO, *Mordechai Schamz.*
JOSHUA COHEN, *Witz.*
EMILY HOLMES COLEMAN, *The Shutter of Snow.*
ERIC CHEVILLARD, *The Author and Me.*
ROBERT COOVER, *A Night at the Movies.*
STANLEY CRAWFORD, *Log of the S.S. The Mrs Unguentine.*
*Some Instructions to My Wife.*
RENÉ CREVEL, *Putting My Foot in It.*
RALPH CUSACK, *Cadenza.*
NICHOLAS DELBANCO, *Sherbrookes.*
*The Count of Concord.*
NIGEL DENNIS, *Cards of Identity.*
PETER DIMOCK, *A Short Rhetoric for Leaving the Family.*
ARIEL DORFMAN, *Konfidenz.*
COLEMAN DOWELL, *Island People.*
*Too Much Flesh and Jabez.*
ARKADII DRAGOMOSHCHENKO, *Dust.*
RIKKI DUCORNET, *Phosphor in Dreamland.*
*The Complete Butcher's Tales.*

RIKKI DUCORNET (cont.), *The Jade Cabinet.*
*The Fountains of Neptune.*
WILLIAM EASTLAKE, *The Bamboo Bed.*
*Castle Keep.*
*Lyric of the Circle Heart.*
JEAN ECHENOZ, *Chopin's Move.*
STANLEY ELKIN, *A Bad Man.*
*Criers and Kibitzers, Kibitzers and Criers.*
*The Dick Gibson Show.*
*The Franchiser.*
*The Living End.*
*Mrs. Ted Bliss.*
FRANÇOIS EMMANUEL, *Invitation to a Voyage.*
PAUL EMOND, *The Dance of a Sham.*
SALVADOR ESPRIU, *Ariadne in the Grotesque Labyrinth.*
LESLIE A. FIEDLER, *Love and Death in the American Novel.*
JUAN FILLOY, *Op Oloop.*
ANDY FITCH, *Pop Poetics.*
GUSTAVE FLAUBERT, *Bouvard and Pécuchet.*
KASS FLEISHER, *Talking out of School.*
JON FOSSE, *Aliss at the Fire.*
*Melancholy.*
FORD MADOX FORD, *The March of Literature.*
MAX FRISCH, *I'm Not Stiller.*
*Man in the Holocene.*
CARLOS FUENTES, *Christopher Unborn.*
*Distant Relations.*
*Terra Nostra.*
*Where the Air Is Clear.*
TAKEHIKO FUKUNAGA, *Flowers of Grass.*
WILLIAM GADDIS, JR., *The Recognitions.*
JANICE GALLOWAY, *Foreign Parts.*
*The Trick Is to Keep Breathing.*
WILLIAM H. GASS, *Life Sentences.*
*The Tunnel.*
*The World Within the Word.*
*Willie Masters' Lonesome Wife.*
GÉRARD GAVARRY, *Hoppla! 1 2 3.*

ETIENNE GILSON, *The Arts of the Beautiful.*
*Forms and Substances in the Arts.*
C. S. GISCOMBE, *Giscome Road.*
*Here.*
DOUGLAS GLOVER, *Bad News of the Heart.*
WITOLD GOMBROWICZ, *A Kind of Testament.*
PAULO EMÍLIO SALES GOMES, *P's Three Women.*
GEORGI GOSPODINOV, *Natural Novel.*
JUAN GOYTISOLO, *Count Julian.*
*Juan the Landless.*
*Makbara.*
*Marks of Identity.*
HENRY GREEN, *Blindness.*
*Concluding.*
*Doting.*
*Nothing.*
JACK GREEN, *Fire the Bastards!*
JIŘÍ GRUŠA, *The Questionnaire.*
MELA HARTWIG, *Am I a Redundant Human Being?*
JOHN HAWKES, *The Passion Artist.*
*Whistlejacket.*
ELIZABETH HEIGHWAY, ED., *Contemporary Georgian Fiction.*
AIDAN HIGGINS, *Balcony of Europe.*
*Blind Man's Bluff.*
*Bornholm Night-Ferry.*
*Langrishe, Go Down.*
*Scenes from a Receding Past.*
KEIZO HINO, *Isle of Dreams.*
KAZUSHI HOSAKA, *Plainsong.*
ALDOUS HUXLEY, *Antic Hay.*
*Point Counter Point.*
*Those Barren Leaves.*
*Time Must Have a Stop.*
NAOYUKI II, *The Shadow of a Blue Cat.*
DRAGO JANČAR, *The Tree with No Name.*
MIKHEIL JAVAKHISHVILI, *Kvachi.*
GERT JONKE, *The Distant Sound.*
*Homage to Czerny.*
*The System of Vienna.*

JACQUES JOUET, *Mountain R*.
*Savage*.
*Upstaged*.
MIEKO KANAI, *The Word Book*.
YORAM KANIUK, *Life on Sandpaper*.
ZURAB KARUMIDZE, *Dagny*.
JOHN KELLY, *From Out of the City*.
HUGH KENNER, *Flaubert, Joyce and Beckett: The Stoic Comedians*.
*Joyce's Voices*.
DANILO KIŠ, *The Attic*.
*The Lute and the Scars*.
*Psalm 44*.
*A Tomb for Boris Davidovich*.
ANITA KONKKA, *A Fool's Paradise*.
GEORGE KONRÁD, *The City Builder*.
TADEUSZ KONWICKI, *A Minor Apocalypse*.
*The Polish Complex*.
ANNA KORDZAIA-SAMADASHVILI, *Me, Margarita*.
MENIS KOUMANDAREAS, *Koula*.
ELAINE KRAF, *The Princess of 72nd Street*.
JIM KRUSOE, *Iceland*.
AYSE KULIN, *Farewell: A Mansion in Occupied Istanbul*.
EMILIO LASCANO TEGUI, *On Elegance While Sleeping*.
ERIC LAURRENT, *Do Not Touch*.
VIOLETTE LEDUC, *La Bâtarde*.
EDOUARD LEVÉ, *Autoportrait*.
*Newspaper*.
*Suicide*.
*Works*.
MARIO LEVI, *Istanbul Was a Fairy Tale*.
DEBORAH LEVY, *Billy and Girl*.
JOSÉ LEZAMA LIMA, *Paradiso*.
ROSA LIKSOM, *Dark Paradise*.
OSMAN LINS, *Avalovara*.
*The Queen of the Prisons of Greece*.
FLORIAN LIPUŠ, *The Errors of Young Tjaž*.
GORDON LISH, *Peru*.
ALF MACLOCHLAINN, *Out of Focus*.
*Past Habitual*.

*The Corpus in the Library*.
RON LOEWINSOHN, *Magnetic Field(s)*.
YURI LOTMAN, *Non-Memoirs*.
D. KEITH MANO, *Take Five*.
MINA LOY, *Stories and Essays of Mina Loy*.
MICHELINE AHARONIAN MARCOM, *A Brief History of Yes*.
*The Mirror in the Well*.
BEN MARCUS, *The Age of Wire and String*.
WALLACE MARKFIELD, *Teitlebaum's Window*.
DAVID MARKSON, *Reader's Block*.
*Wittgenstein's Mistress*.
CAROLE MASO, *AVA*.
HISAKI MATSUURA, *Triangle*.
LADISLAV MATEJKA & KRYSTYNA POMORSKA, EDS., *Readings in Russian Poetics: Formalist & Structuralist Views*.
HARRY MATHEWS, *Cigarettes*.
*The Conversions*.
*The Human Country*.
*The Journalist*.
*My Life in CIA*.
*Singular Pleasures*.
*The Sinking of the Odradek Stadium*.
*Tlooth*.
HISAKI MATSUURA, *Triangle*.
DONAL MCLAUGHLIN, *beheading the virgin mary, and other stories*.
JOSEPH MCELROY, *Night Soul and Other Stories*.
ABDELWAHAB MEDDEB, *Talismano*.
GERHARD MEIER, *Isle of the Dead*.
HERMAN MELVILLE, *The Confidence-Man*.
AMANDA MICHALOPOULOU, *I'd Like*.
STEVEN MILLHAUSER, *The Barnum Museum*.
*In the Penny Arcade*.
RALPH J. MILLS, JR., *Essays on Poetry*.
MOMUS, *The Book of Jokes*.
CHRISTINE MONTALBETTI, *The Origin of Man*.
*Western*.

NICHOLAS MOSLEY, *Accident.*
*Assassins.*
*Catastrophe Practice.*
*A Garden of Trees.*
*Hopeful Monsters.*
*Imago Bird.*
*Inventing God.*
*Look at the Dark.*
*Metamorphosis.*
*Natalie Natalia.*
*Serpent.*

WARREN MOTTE, *Fables of the Novel: French Fiction since 1990.*
*Fiction Now: The French Novel in the 21st Century.*
*Mirror Gazing.*
*Oulipo: A Primer of Potential Literature.*

GERALD MURNANE, *Barley Patch.*
*Inland.*

YVES NAVARRE, *Our Share of Time.*
*Sweet Tooth.*

DOROTHY NELSON, *In Night's City.*
*Tar and Feathers.*

ESHKOL NEVO, *Homesick.*

WILFRIDO D. NOLLEDO, *But for the Lovers.*

BORIS A. NOVAK, *The Master of Insomnia.*

FLANN O'BRIEN, *At Swim-Two-Birds.*
*The Best of Myles.*
*The Dalkey Archive.*
*The Hard Life.*
*The Poor Mouth.*
*The Third Policeman.*

CLAUDE OLLIER, *The Mise-en-Scène.*
*Wert and the Life Without End.*

PATRIK OUŘEDNÍK, *Europeana.*
*The Opportune Moment, 1855.*

BORIS PAHOR, *Necropolis.*

FERNANDO DEL PASO, *News from the Empire.*
*Palinuro of Mexico.*

ROBERT PINGET, *The Inquisitory.*
*Mahu or The Material.*
*Trio.*

MANUEL PUIG, *Betrayed by Rita Hayworth.*

*The Buenos Aires Affair.*
*Heartbreak Tango.*

RAYMOND QUENEAU, *The Last Days.*
*Odile.*
*Pierrot Mon Ami.*
*Saint Glinglin.*

ANN QUIN, *Berg.*
*Passages.*
*Three.*
*Tripticks.*

ISHMAEL REED, *The Free-Lance Pallbearers.*
*The Last Days of Louisiana Red.*
*Ishmael Reed: The Plays.*
*Juice!*
*The Terrible Threes.*
*The Terrible Twos.*
*Yellow Back Radio Broke-Down.*

JASIA REICHARDT, *15 Journeys Warsaw to London.*

JOÃO UBALDO RIBEIRO, *House of the Fortunate Buddhas.*

JEAN RICARDOU, *Place Names.*

RAINER MARIA RILKE,
*The Notebooks of Malte Laurids Brigge.*

JULIÁN RÍOS, *The House of Ulysses.*
*Larva: A Midsummer Night's Babel.*
*Poundemonium.*

ALAIN ROBBE-GRILLET, *Project for a Revolution in New York.*
*A Sentimental Novel.*

AUGUSTO ROA BASTOS, *I the Supreme.*

DANIËL ROBBERECHTS, *Arriving in Avignon.*

JEAN ROLIN, *The Explosion of the Radiator Hose.*

OLIVIER ROLIN, *Hotel Crystal.*

ALIX CLEO ROUBAUD, *Alix's Journal.*

JACQUES ROUBAUD, *The Form of a City Changes Faster, Alas, Than the Human Heart.*
*The Great Fire of London.*
*Hortense in Exile.*
*Hortense Is Abducted.*
*Mathematics: The Plurality of Worlds of Lewis.*
*Some Thing Black.*

RAYMOND ROUSSEL, *Impressions of Africa.*

VEDRANA RUDAN, *Night.*

PABLO M. RUIZ, *Four Cold Chapters on the Possibility of Literature.*

GERMAN SADULAEV, *The Maya Pill.*

TOMAŽ ŠALAMUN, *Soy Realidad.*

LYDIE SALVAYRE, *The Company of Ghosts.*
*The Lecture.*
*The Power of Flies.*

LUIS RAFAEL SÁNCHEZ, *Macho Camacho's Beat.*

SEVERO SARDUY, *Cobra & Maitreya.*

NATHALIE SARRAUTE, *Do You Hear Them?*
*Martereau.*
*The Planetarium.*

STIG SÆTERBAKKEN, *Siamese.*
*Self-Control.*
*Through the Night.*

ARNO SCHMIDT, *Collected Novellas.*
*Collected Stories.*
*Nobodaddy's Children.*
*Two Novels.*

ASAF SCHURR, *Motti.*

GAIL SCOTT, *My Paris.*

DAMION SEARLS, *What We Were Doing and Where We Were Going.*

JUNE AKERS SEESE, *Is This What Other Women Feel Too?*

BERNARD SHARE, *Inish.*
*Transit.*

VIKTOR SHKLOVSKY, *Bowstring.*
*Literature and Cinematography.*
*Theory of Prose.*
*Third Factory.*
*Zoo, or Letters Not about Love.*

PIERRE SINIAC, *The Collaborators.*

KJERSTI A. SKOMSVOLD, *The Faster I Walk, the Smaller I Am.*

JOSEF ŠKVORECKÝ, *The Engineer of Human Souls.*

GILBERT SORRENTINO, *Aberration of Starlight.*
*Blue Pastoral.*
*Crystal Vision.*

*Imaginative Qualities of Actual Things.*
*Mulligan Stew. Red the Fiend.*
*Steelwork.*
*Under the Shadow.*

MARKO SOSIČ, *Ballerina, Ballerina.*

ANDRZEJ STASIUK, *Dukla.*
*Fado.*

GERTRUDE STEIN, *The Making of Americans.*
*A Novel of Thank You.*

LARS SVENDSEN, *A Philosophy of Evil.*

PIOTR SZEWC, *Annihilation.*

GONÇALO M. TAVARES, *A Man: Klaus Klump.*
*Jerusalem.*
*Learning to Pray in the Age of Technique.*

LUCIAN DAN TEODOROVICI, *Our Circus Presents . . .*

NIKANOR TERATOLOGEN, *Assisted Living.*

STEFAN THEMERSON, *Hobson's Island.*
*The Mystery of the Sardine.*
*Tom Harris.*

TAEKO TOMIOKA, *Building Waves.*

JOHN TOOMEY, *Sleepwalker.*

DUMITRU TSEPENEAG, *Hotel Europa.*
*The Necessary Marriage.*
*Pigeon Post.*
*Vain Art of the Fugue.*

ESTHER TUSQUETS, *Stranded.*

DUBRAVKA UGRESIC, *Lend Me Your Character.*
*Thank You for Not Reading.*

TOR ULVEN, *Replacement.*

MATI UNT, *Brecht at Night.*
*Diary of a Blood Donor.*
*Things in the Night.*

ÁLVARO URIBE & OLIVIA SEARS, EDS., *Best of Contemporary Mexican Fiction.*

ELOY URROZ, *Friction.*
*The Obstacles.*

LUISA VALENZUELA, *Dark Desires and the Others.*
*He Who Searches.*

PAUL VERHAEGHEN, *Omega Minor.*

BORIS VIAN, *Heartsnatcher.*

LLORENÇ VILLALONGA, *The Dolls' Room.*

TOOMAS VINT, *An Unending Landscape.*

ORNELA VORPSI, *The Country Where No One Ever Dies.*

AUSTRYN WAINHOUSE, *Hedyphagetica.*

CURTIS WHITE, *America's Magic Mountain.*
*The Idea of Home.*
*Memories of My Father Watching TV.*
*Requiem.*

DIANE WILLIAMS,
*Excitability: Selected Stories.*
*Romancer Erector.*

DOUGLAS WOOLF, *Wall to Wall.*
*Ya! & John-Juan.*

JAY WRIGHT, *Polynomials and Pollen.*
*The Presentable Art of Reading Absence.*

PHILIP WYLIE, *Generation of Vipers.*

MARGUERITE YOUNG, *Angel in the Forest.*
*Miss MacIntosh, My Darling.*

REYOUNG, *Unbabbling.*

VLADO ŽABOT, *The Succubus.*

ZORAN ŽIVKOVIĆ , *Hidden Camera.*

LOUIS ZUKOFSKY, *Collected Fiction.*

VITOMIL ZUPAN, *Minuet for Guitar.*

SCOTT ZWIREN, *God Head.*

*AND MORE . . .*